Guido Vitale

Chinese Folklore

Pekinese rhymes

Guido Vitale

Chinese Folklore
Pekinese rhymes

ISBN/EAN: 9783337264413

Printed in Europe, USA, Canada, Australia, Japan

Cover: Foto ©Andreas Hilbeck / pixelio.de

More available books at **www.hansebooks.com**

CHINESE FOLKLORE

PEKINESE RHYMES

FIRST COLLECTED AND EDITED WITH

NOTES AND TRANSLATION

BY

BARON GUIDO VITALE

CHINESE SECRETARY TO THE ITALIAN LEGATION.

PEKING.

PEI-T'ANG PRESS

1896.

TO

PROFESSOR LODOVICO NOCENTINI

IN

SIGN OF ESTEEM AND FRIENDSHIP

PREFACE

I bring for the first time to light a collection of Pekinese children-rhymes with the conviction that the reader may gather from the lecture these benefits.

1°. The acquirement of a small treasure of words and phrases hardly to be met with elsewhere.

2°. A clearer insight into scenes and details of chinese common life.

3°. The notion that some true poetry may be found in chinese popular songs.

These rhymes have no known authors; some of them are perhaps composed by mothers watching at children's bedside, others may be composed by naughty school-boys when the teacher is having his nap over a page of the great philosopher. At all events they are like wild flowers which spring up nobody knows how and when and fade and die in the same way.

The trouble in collecting them was far greater than I had thought. "Tabood" as we are in Peking, where could I go myself to hear the rhymes and note them down?

Then I had recourse to my teacher, but as he thinks to be a literary man, he grew quite indignant at my proposal, and assured and pledged that no such rubbish had ever existed in China. However as I happened (of course by chance) to take out of my drawer some dollars, and place them beneath his reach, he suddenly abated his furors and mumbled that "perhaps I was not mistaken and that of course he would by every possible mean try to get what I wanted".

And I shall say to his justice that he kept his word and the dollars. But when he had collected forty or so, his stock was quite exhausted and I had to look for other helps.

In summer time residing in temples in the neighbourhood of Peking I had large chance of intercourse with the people and could increase my stock of rhymes. I was furthermore able to improve the former texts and to reprove all those which being not matched by oral testimony were probably spurious.

After the work of collection, came the work of explanation and translation which was not always easy. The people who spoke the words often were not able to give me light on the difficult points. When pressed by me they suggested something and I picked up what looked more truthlike and reasonable; never did I force or prefer views of my own.

Somebody will object to my statement that sparkles of true poetry are to be found in this book. That will very naturally happen to all those who are entirely foreign to the chinese world. Several rhymes (however few in proportion to the bulk of the book)[1] are simple and touching and may be "poetry" for those who have even a slight knowledge of chinese joys and sorrows.

I shall draw also the reader's attention to the system of versification followed in these rhymes. Composed as they are by illiterate people who have no notion of written language, they show a system of versification analogous to that of many European countries, and almost completely agreeing with the rules

---

[1] 3.9.10.11.13.15.23.32.43.44.53.54.55.60.91.117.123.125.

of the Italian poetry. A new national poetry could perhaps spring up based on these rhythms and on the true feelings of the people.

I took every pain to collect the most I could, yet the work could be by far richer than it is. Those who live in freeer intercourse with the people could easily add numerous and fine samples of this uncultivated poetry. I would be extremely pleased if any one would either furnish to me new materials, or would himself undertake the work of a new collection of rhymes.

Any critic, advise or literary contribution will be gratefully received by the author.

I am glad to be able to express here my deep feelings of gratitude to Mr. A. M. C. Raab of the British Legation, who kindly undertook the revision of almost the whole manuscript and to Mr. Krebs of the German Legation who kindly helped me in correcting the proofs.

BARON GUIDO VITALE

Italian Legation.

Peking. 30th September 1896.

INDEX.

PEKING. — Pei-t'ang Press.

PEKINESE BABY-SONGS

I

鋸　大　拉
鋸　大　扯
頭　木　鋸
子　房　蓋
家　姥　姥
子　娘　娶

棚　大　搭
戲　大　唱
娘　姑　接
婿　女　請
甥　外　小
去　也　你

NOTES

Singing these words, the mother or any elder of the family takes the baby by the hands and pushes him for and backwards as if it was really the matter of drawing a saw. 姥姥家 lao³ lao³ chia¹, the family of the mother's mother. 娶娘子 ch'ü³ niang²-tzŭ, goes to fetch the bride for her son, niang²-tzŭ is the name for a wife, and here it is used instead of 新姑娘 hsin¹-ku¹-niang², the real term for a bride. 搭大棚 ta¹-ta¹-p'eng², they raise a large matshed. The chinese houses have not generally large rooms, therefore in marriage, death, anniversary, and other occasions in which many guests are to be invited.

an additional matshed is raised in the court-yard. 大戲 tá-hsī, a play performed in the matshed by hired actors, an amusement much liked by the Chinese, but which only rich people can afford to have in their houses. 接姑娘請女婿 chie¹ ku¹-niang¹ ch'ing³ nü³-hsü⁴, the grandmother with her family invites on this marriage occasion her married daughters and their husbands. 外甥 uai⁴-sheng¹, is the name by which a sister's son is designed.

TRANSLATION

(People) draw the saw — pull the saw — saw the wood — build rooms — the grandmother and her family go to fetch the bride — a large mat-shed is raised — in which a play is performed — and they come to take home the married daughters — and to invite their husbands — small nephew — do you want also to go?

II

台 轆 軸 上
台 轆 軸 下
張 家 媽 媽 倒 茶 來
茶 也 香
酒 也 香

裳水腿惱到　拉家家兒去　飯

衣駝口褲別來　馬人褂兒等阿那親我老茶兒　的老包牙

駝駝一花你車　車個銀針二間上瞧到的奶四物兒

駱動着姐姐兒　轎着襖包了門煞邊親成檳榔這

個動愣含小小後車轆坐皮荷來車阿南了現醇檳

八不麻愣了姐兒轂頭鼠子南着煞到完家子南你

十駝叫麻噴小明甚紅裏灰對解把阿我瞧我達安硌

NOTES

軲轆台 ku¹ lu¹ t'ai², a rounded stone placed Some times outside the outerdoors to sit on. 麻愣 ma²-leng⁴ is the dragon fly (libellula virgo); it ought to be correctly written 螞螂 and pronounced ma[1]-lang[2], I have however preferred the more popular and incorrect form as the sounds and the tones of the characters correspond to the Pekinese pronunciation, and the correct form is popularly unknown. 含着 hen[2]-cho, holding something in the mouth without showing it. The correct pronunciation of the character 含 is han[2], as it is also pronounced in vulgar phrases as for instance 暗含着 an[4] han[2] cho, hiddenly, without showing, said sometimes of a meaning hidden in words which pretend not to say anything. 褲腿 k'u[4] t'uei[3], cloth-bands wrapped around the ankles of ladies with small feet. 轎車 chiao[4] ch'o[1], sort of cart longer than the ordinary one, used only by the upper mandarin classes. 俏人家 ch'iao[1] jen[2] chia[1], a beautiful woman. 灰鼠 huei[1]-shu[3], the grey squirrel. 皮襖 p'i[2]-ao[3], chinese overcoat lined with fur. 銀鼠 yin[2]-shu[3], the white squirrel. 對子 tuei[4]-tzu, a pair; the numeral — one is wanting. 荷包 ho[2]-pao[1], a small side-pouch in which the chinese keep banknotes, or even betel-nuts. 小針兒 hsiao[3]-chen[1]-eur, a small needle used by women to work flowers on a cloth. This working different from the embroidery is called 扎 cha[1]. 轄 hsia[1], the character ought to be pronounced in the second tone, but here is pronounced in the first because it is only used to represent the Manchu word hiyà meaning a body-guard of the sovereign; this word is very often used in Peking instead of the chinese equivalent 侍衛 shih[4]-wei[4]. 阿綹 a[1]-sha[1], two

characters which represent the Manchu word *asha*
meaning one's elder brother's wife, and is used in the
same complimentary way and in the same meaning
as the chinese 嫂子 sao³-tzŭ. 達子餑餑 ta²-tzŭ puo¹-
puo¹, tartar-cakes many of which keep yet their old
Manchu names, and are largely used in Peking.
奶茶 nai³-ch'a², "milk-tea". 安南檳榔 an¹-nan²-
ping¹-lang², Annamite betel-nuts. 夾四瓣兒 chia¹-
ssu⁴-pan⁴ 'r, which are cut in four pieces. 硌 ko⁴
character not mentioned in any dictionary; it means
to stick in the teeth, and also to hinder, to hurt.
厭物兒 yen⁴ u⁴ 'r, despising term for a person who
disgusts people; it could be translated " you
worrying thing!" 包牙 pao¹ ya², it is said of the
front teeth when they protrude under the upper lip.

TRANSLATION

Goes up the sitting-stone — comes down from
the sitting stone (!). The old lady Chang comes to
pour tea — the tea is fragrant — the wine is fragrant
— ten camels are loaden with clothes — they are
unable to move on — and they call the dragon-fly
— the dragon fly-with the mouth full of water —
spurts the young lady's figured ankle-bands — young
lady, young lady do not get cross — to-morrow or
after to-morrow the cart shall arrive — what cart?
— a chair-cart with red wheels, drawn by a white
horse — and inside there sits a beautiful woman —
who wears an over coat lined with grey squirrel

fur and a jacket lined with ermine fur — and has
with her a pair of side-pouches with flowers worked
on it by the small needle — then, comes from the
south direction an Imperial body-guard of the
second class — who leaning to the cart-door asks
his sister-in-law — sister-in-law, sister-in law,
where do you go? — "I am going towards South
to pay a visit to my family" — "When you have
already paid a visit to your family, come to my
house. — I have at home ready-cooked old rice —
tartar cakes and tea milk — but the Annamite betel-
nuts cut in four pieces — shall break the protruding
old front teeth of you worrying thing!"

III

楊 樹 葉 兒
嘩 拉 拉
小 孩 兒 睡 覺 找 他 媽
乖 乖 寶 貝 兒 你 睡 罷
螞 虎 子 來 了 我 打 他

NOTES

楊樹 yang² shu⁴, the poplar (latin *populus*) this
tree is in China very commonly seen in burial
grounds. The Chinese say that its leaves stir even

without wind, and that the noise produced by their stirring, moves to sadness. 嘩拉拉 hua¹ la¹ là¹, pronounced as one word, is imitative of the noise. This sad introduction is supposed to scare the boy and to get him sooner asleep. 乖乖 kuai¹-kuai¹, means to kiss as chinese mothers kiss their children in somewat a different way than the Europeans. The same expression is used too to say : be quiet! dont be saucy! — probably the two meanings melt in one, as the second may simply be a promise of a kiss if the boy will be quiet. Another common form for the last meaning is adverbially formed so, 乖乖兒的 kuai¹ kuai¹'r ti. 蟆虎子 ma¹ hu³ tzŭ, a phantastic monstruos creature spoken of and called every time it is thought proper to scare a baby.

TRANSLATION

The poplar leaves — are stirring — the baby is about to sleep and looks for his mother — be a good boy, my treasure, get asleep — if the bogie comes, I'll beat him.

IV

桃 水 的 哥
聽 着 我 說
南 河 沿 兒

有 你 的 窩
晴 天 哂 蓋 子
陰 天 把 脖 兒 縮

NOTES

These words are adressed by the chinese boys to the water-carriers who are generally people of the Shantung province. As no water-ways of any kind exist in Peking, a great many of these fellows take the water from the wells into the houses. Their bad pronunciation, and their awkward manners delight extremely the Peking cockneys. The boys have therefore composed for their benefit this special song, which they hum at their back, and whose general aim is to define them as turtles. The word turtle in China is used for one of the most direst insults, as this animal is phantastically empeached of an unnatural crime. The insult is however so largely used that people are not shocked by it. 哥 ko¹ means elder brother, but here is used in the meaning of man, fellow in the same way as the Russians use the word brat (latin *frater*). 窩 uo¹ means not only a nest but also a den, a hole. 哂 蓋 子 shai¹ kai⁴- tzŭ, to dry the shell in the sun, as turtles do. 縮 suo¹, to withdraw one's head, to retreat. This last phrase is allusive to the fact that the water-carriers do not go out when it rains, as the turtles do too.

TRANSLATION

Water carrying fellow — hear what I say — on the bank of the south river — is your hole — when the weather is fine, you dry out your shell — and when it is bad weather then you draw in your neck.

V

沙 土 地 兒
跑 白 馬
一 跑 跑 到 丈 人 家
大 舅 兒 望 裏 讓
小 舅 兒 望 裏 拉
隔 着 竹 簾 兒 看 見 他
銀 盤 大 臉 黑 頭 髮
月 白 緞 子 棉 襖 銀 疙 疸

NOTES

沙 土 地 兒 sha¹ t'u³ ti⁴r, a sandy plain ground as outside the wall between the Manchu and the Chinese town in Peking. 丈 人 chang⁴-jen, name given to one's wife or bride's father. 大 舅 兒 ta⁴-chiou⁴'r, one's wife's elder brother. 小 舅 兒 hsiao³ chiou⁴'r, one's wife's younger brother. For 他 is here to be understood the bride whom the young man succeeds in spying through the curtain. 銀 盤 大

臉 yin² p'an² ta⁴ lien³, a big face as white as a silver tray. 月白 yüe⁴ pai², "moon white" means a light blue. 疙疸 read ko¹-ta¹ or more vulgarly ka¹-ta¹, here means a metal button, it may also mean pimples and has other different shades of meanings.

TRANSLATION

On the sandy plain — gallops a white horse — galloping gets to the (horseman's) future father-in-law's house — his elder brother-in-law invites him to come in — his younger brother-in-law pulls him in — through the bamboo-curtain he has seen her — her large face as white as a silver-tray and her black hair — and her cotton overcoat of light azure colour with silver buttons.

VI

小禿兒
咧咧咧
南邊兒打水是你爹
你爹戴着紅纓帽
你媽穿着乍板兒鞋
走一步
蹋拉拉
十個脚指頭露着三

NOTES

The chinese boys generally as far as three years old have their hair shaven; therefore a common nickname for a boy is 禿兒 t'u¹¹r, meaning a bald-headed. 咧咧咧 lie¹-lie¹-lie¹, is imitative of the sound of weeping. The boy weeps and to quiet him the song is sung to him. 打水 ta³ shuei³, to draw water from a well, by a rope and a bucket. 紅纓子 hung² ing¹ tzǔ, Red silk twists fixed round the top of a chinese official hat. 乍板兒鞋 cha⁴ pan³'r hsie², old shoes with no heels; they are so called because the noise the sole produces slapping on the ground is like the sound of a chinese musical instrument called 乍板兒 cha⁴ pan³'r, consisting in two small bamboo tablets strung together, which are shaken by the fingers in a similar manner to the spanish and italian castanets 蹋拉拉 t'a¹ la¹ la¹, imitates the slapping of the shoe sole on the ground. 三 san¹ is here (as very often in vulgar language) pronounced sa¹, in order to rhyme with the precedent verse who ends with 拉.

TRANSLATION

Small bald-headed — here he is weeping! — to the South side it's your father who draws water from the well — your father wears an official hat with red silk twists on it — and your mother wears on her feet old shoes with no heels — as she advances a step — it sounds t'alalà — and of her ten toes three peep out of her shoes.

VII

麻子麻
上樹爬
狗叉咬
人叉拿
嚇的麻子摔了個麻跟頭
麻大錢
買了個麻燒餅
麻子吃
麻子看
麻子打架麻子勸
麻衙役
拿板子
單打麻子的麻腿子

NOTES

This song is profusedly interspersed with the character 麻 ma² whose meaning is "small pox." This disease is so common in China that very often children who have been sick with it and keep marks on their faces are familiarly called 瘢子 ma²-tzŭ. Furthermore the word is used in other relative meanings. Here throughout these words, it is impossible to translate it always, as the repetition is done for the sake of playing on the word. The character I have written here is the regular one, but popularly the other character 麻 ma², which means hemp, is substituted for it. In the first verse it is repeated to intensify the original meaning, thus saying "much marked with small pox." 瘢 跟頭 ma² ken¹ t'ou², ken¹-t'ou² is a tumble; the word 瘢 ma² is referred to the subject. 麻大錢 ma² ta¹ ch'ien², so is called a cash when its surface is sugged, uneven, as if there were marks of small pox on it. 麻燒餅 ma² shao¹ ping³, a wheaten cake with an uneven surface, as it is when sesamum seeds are placed on it. 燒餅 shao¹ ping³, round wheaten cake.

TRANSLATION

The boy much marked with the small pox — climbs up a tree — the dog barks — and people go to catch him. — The small-pox marked is so scared that he tumbles. — With an old rugged cash he buys a cake — a small pox marked eats — and a small pox marked looks on — the small pox marked come to a fight — and a small-pox marked advises peace — small pox marked policemen — take the bamboo stick — and only thrash the legs of the small pox marked boy.

VIII

兒

頑兒燒苦腐爛蛋雞坐出坐出鼻子

我鐮兒瓜苦腐爛雞蛋頭哥頭奶了

跟火鐮甜瓜豆腐雞蛋頭哥頭奶了

誰打火賣甜賣豆茶雞裏哥哥裏奶奶燒

雞坐出坐出鼻子

蛋著來着來子

殼哥買奶燒眼

殼哥茶奶香晴

NOTES

火鐮兒 huo³ lien²'r, a piece of steel used to strike sparks from a flint. 甜瓜 t'ien² kua¹, sweet melon. 豆腐 tou⁴-fu³, bean cheese, largely used in China 茶雞蛋 ch'a² chi¹ tan⁴, eggs boiled in tea. 雞蛋殼兒 chi¹ tan⁴ k'o¹'r the shell of an egg; it is generally pronounced k'o²'r.

TRANSLATION

Who is going to play with me? — strike the flint-steel — the flint steel takes fire — sell sweet melons — the sweet melons are bitter — sell bean cheese — the bean cheese is spoiled — boil eggs in tea — in the shell of the egg, of the egg — there is sitting the elder brother — the elder brother goes out to buy provisions — inside there sits the grand-mother — the grand mother goes out to burn incense — and burns her nose and her eyes.

IX

我 一 個 大 兒 子
一 個 兒 子
寶 貝 疙 疸 兒
開 胸 順 氣 丸

NOTES

These words are often repeated by the pekinese mothers to their babies 疙 疸 兒 ko¹ ta¹ 'r, means here a little thing of a round form just as it was a round metal button. 開 胸 順 氣 丸 k'ai¹ hsiung¹ shun⁴ ch'i¹ uan², is a medical pill advised by chinese doctors to people who feel the breast oppressed and the respiration uneasy. The literal translation of its name is "pill which opens (lightens) the breast and makes the respiration easy. The mothers liken their babies to that pill, and really every mother holding her child in her arms must feel happy and free from every sorrow.

TRANSLATION.

This one great son of mine! — one son of mine! a precious little thing! — a pill who lightens the heart and makes people happy!

X

我 兒 子 睡 覺 了
我 花 兒 困 覺 了
我 花 兒 把 卜 了
我 花 兒 是 個 乖 兒 子
我 花 兒 是 個 哄 人 精

NOTES

These words are repeated by mothers near the cradles of their sons to get them asleep. The phrase 把卜了 pa⁴ pu³ la, is rather difficult to explain, because the Chinese themselves cannot give it a meaning. However, after many enquiries I see that people are generally of opinion that this phrase has the meaning of being drowsy, being asleep. 乖兒子 kuai¹ eur² tzŭ, an obedient boy, meaning derived from the above mentioned phrase 乖乖 kuai¹ kuai¹, "be quiet!" 哄人的精 hung³ jen² ti ching¹, the word hung³ which means commonly to deceive, but its original meaning is to cajole, to flatter, to charm. The word ching¹ means essence, semen; the whole phrase could be translated: the essence, the flower of those who charm people.

TRANSLATION

My flower is sleeping — my flower has fallen asleep — my flower is resting — my flower is a quiet son — my flower is the flower of those who charm people.

XI

看梅花了家擀麵片
你探梅花沒探到我會一線團團花瓣
狗邊花兒媳婦擀麵賽寨裏如團蓮花轉瓣
黄南梅人媳擀刀鍋裏碗裏
狗到朶雙家起起在在
黄我一雙我拿拿掤盛

?

碗

一碗兩碗

半碗一碗

碗碗舔了上

瞪着眼直在那兒睡

一藏舔砸鋸兒媳裏

婆姑下來舔砸鋸兒媳睡

碗底過過過媳兒坑甚麼皮甚麼皮甚麼錘

一個板兒兒子的婦爐甚羊甚狗甚棒

公兩案貓狗耗嚇媳在鋪鋪蓋蓋枕枕

公公拿着一落磚

婆婆拿着一溜鞭

打的媳婦兒一溜烟

NOTES

This song although very childish, yet is founded on the fact that chinese mothers-in-law are often unkind and sometimes even cruel to their daughters-in-law. 雙雙人兒 shuang[1] shuang[1] jen[2]'r, means a couple of persons, not four persons. 我家媳婦兒 uo[3] chia[1] hsi[2] fu[4]'r, "the wife in my house" probably these words are meant to be uttered by the mother in law, who may call so her son's daughter. 擀麪 kan³ mien⁴, to stretch out dough to make vermicelli. 擀麪杖 kan³ mien⁴ chang⁴, a roller to stretch dough. — 大 片 i¹ ta⁴ p'ien⁴, a large flat piece (of dough); in the text the verb "she stretches out" is wanting. 賽如線 sai⁴ ju⁴ hsien⁴, which may rival, compete with thread as to thinness. 團團轉 t'uan² t'uan² chuan⁴, conglomerated they turn round in the pan. (said of the vermicelli) 蓮花瓣 lien²-hua¹-pan⁴, (as they were) petals of the lotus blossom. 公 kung¹ father-in-law, here kung¹ is instead of 公公 kung¹ kung¹. 婆 p'uo², mother in law, here p'uo² is instead of 婆婆 p'uo² p'uo². 小姑兒 hsiao³ ku¹'r, her husband's younger sisters. 案板 an⁴ pan³, a wood board on which dough is stretched to make vermicelli. 爐坑 lu² k'eng¹ is a pit under the stove where the ashes fall down; an imcommon severe punishment inflicted by mothers-in-law to their daughters-in-law is to let them sleep in the stove-pit. 鋪甚麼 p'u¹ she² mmo, what have you for bedding? 枕甚麼 chen³ she² mmo, what have you for pillow? Somebody is supposed to ask now from the unfortunate wife about her condition. 棒鎚 pang⁴ ch'ui², a beater used in washing clothes; it is generally made of 棗木 tsao³ mu⁴, date wood. — 落磚 i¹ luo⁴ chuan¹, a pile of bricks, that is to say, as many bricks as could form a pile of them. — 溜鞭 i¹ liou⁴ pien¹, "a row of whips" rather a strange expression for many whips, lots of whips. — 溜烟 i¹ liou⁴ yen¹, as a stream of smoke; the verse is not complete because its whole meaning is : they beat the wife so that she runs away as quickly as a stream of smoke (a cloud of smoke). The Chinese associate the idea of smoke with quickness; very often it is heard 他 走 一 溜 烟 兒 似 的 t'a¹ tsou³ i¹ liou⁴ yen¹'r shih⁴-ti, he walks as quickly as a stream of smoke.

.

TRANSLATION

Yellow dog, yellow dog, look after the house — I go towards South to pluck plum-blossoms — I have not yet plucked a single plum-blossom — and two persons arrive at the house — my son's wife knows how to stretch out dough — she takes the roller and stretches a large slice of dough — she takes the knife and cuts vermicelli as thin as hread — then she puts them in the cooking-pan, and they turn conglomerated about — afterwards she puts them down in the bowls and they look like petals of the lotus blossom. — (She fills) one bowl for her father-in-law — one bowl for her mother-in-law — and two half-bowls for her sisters-in-law — she hides one bowl under the dough-board — but the cat comes over and licks the bowl — the dog comes over and has broken the bowl — the mice come over and gnaw the bowl — and the housewife is so scared that she stares vacantly — " wife, wife, where do you sleep ? " — "I sleep in the stove-pit — what have you for bedding ? — I have for bedding a goat's skin — what have you for coverlet ? — I have a dog's skin — what have you for pillow ? — I have a linen-beater — the father-in-law takes up in his hands as many bricks as could form a pile — the mother-in-law holds up in her hands a row of whips — and they beat the wife so that she runs away as quickly as a stream of smoke.

XII

寒 鴉 兒 寒 鴉 兒 過
一 遍 打 十 個
熬 着 吃
煑 着 吃
剝 了 皮 兒 更 好 吃

NOTES

寒 鴉 兒 han² ya''r' is the Corvus monedula, a white breasted crow; a large number of them comes to Peking from the North, at the beginning of winter, and their first apparition is greeted by the Pekinese boys with these verses who are however too gastronomic to be sentimental. The flesh of these crows is eatable, but the taste for it is not general. — 遍 i¹ pien⁴, at one time. 剝 puo¹ is read vulgarly pao².

TRANSLATION

The white breasted crows, the white breasted crows are passing — at one time we strike ten of them — we eat them boiled in gravy — we eat them boiled — but they are even better to eat when the skin is taken off them.

XIII

小白菜兒
地裏黃兒
七八歲兒
離了娘兒
好好兒跟着爹爹過
又怕爹爹娶後娘
娶了後娘三年整
養了個兄弟比我強
他吃菜
我泡湯
哭哭啼啼想親娘

NOTES

Of all the popular songs that are in this collection, I think this one could claim any artistic value. It is very simple, subject and words, but the child's grief is movingly depicted. The boy likenes himself to a small cabbage which gets yellow and dry in the earth, because nobody takes care of it. The comparison is not poetical for us, but in China there is nothing peculiarly vulgar attached to the word cabbage. 過 kuo¹ is here for 過 日 子 kuo¹ jih¹-tzŭ, to live, to get on. 三 年 整 san¹ nien² cheng³, just after three years. 泡 湯 p'ao¹ t'ang¹, to pour ? the gravy on the rice. 哭 哭 啼 啼 k'u¹ k'u¹ t'i² t'i², weeping and wailing.

TRANSLATION

Like the small cabbage — which has become yellow and dry on the ground — at the age of seven or eight years, I have lost my mother. — I lived so well near my father — only I was afraid he would take another wife — and he has taken her; just after three years — they have given me a brother who is more worthy than I am — because he eats the food — and I only may pour the gravy on my rice — weeping and wailing I think of my own mother!

XIV

張 大 嫂
李 大 嫂

上南坡角
摘豆角
肚子疼
往家跑
撩炕蓆
鋪炕草
養了個兒子
叫豆保
豆保開大店
又賣饅頭又賣麨

NOTES

大嫂 ta[4] sao[3], general appellation for the eldest brother's wife; married women call each other ta[4] sao[3] for sake of ceremony. 豆角 tou[4] chiao[3], bean pods. 撩 liao[1], to grasp, to pull, here, "to pull away" 炕蓆 k'ang[4] hsi[2], the mat wich is spread on the k'ang. Somebody could be curious to know which of the two ladies ran home, but the song does not satisfy the curiosity.

TRANSLATION

Mistress Chang — and Mistress Li — have gone to the Southern slope — to gather bean pods — (one of them) felt a pain in her bosom — and ran home — pulled off the k'ang-mat — spread dry grass on the k'ang — and bore a child whom she called Tou[1] pao[3] — Tou[1]-pao[3] not it has opened a shop — and sells bread and flower.

XV

日頭出來一點紅
師傳騎馬我騎龍
師傳騎馬遠街走
我騎青龍過海東
海東有着家盆花
我家種個五芍藥
大姐愛個紅丹花
二姐愛的牡桃蓮
三姐愛的是大愛
四姐愛的姐的　辮花
剩下五出兒陶氣
一心要人受婆熬
出家人不受夫于
一來不不中抱遙
二來不懷淡逍
三來懷散
四來散

NOTES

芍藥 shao[3] yao[1], peony, lat. *pæonia* 牡丹 mu[3] tan[1],

the tree peony, lat. *pæonia mutan.* 蓮花, lien² hua¹, the lotus flower, lat. *Nelumbium speciosum.* 無的愛 u² ti¹ ai⁴, she has nothing that she likes. 出家 ch'u¹ chia¹, "to go out of the family" means to enter the monastic life. 樂陶陶 lo⁴ t'ao² t'ao², joyfully, happily. 熬 ao¹, to boil, to decoct, and figurately to vex, to disturb. 散淡 san³ tan⁴, freely, easily, with no coercions 逍遙 hsiao¹ yao², in a state of peace and bliss.

TRANSLATION

The sun has come out like a red spot — my teacher rides on a horse and I ride on a dragon — the teacher riding on the horse goes along the streets — I riding on the dark dragon cross over to the East of the sea — at the East of the sea there lives my family — and in my family they cultivate five fllower-pots — my first sister likes the red peony — my second sister likes the tree peony — my third sister likes the petals of the peach blossom — my fourth sister likes the large lotus blossoms. — There is the fifth sister who has nothing she may like — and does not think of other but of becoming a nun — the women in the monastic life live very happily indeed -- firstly they do not suffer the vexations of father-and mother-in-law -- secondly they do not suffer a husband's maltreatment — thirdly they do not bear children — and fourthly they live freely and in a condition of blissful peace.

剔 燈 棍 兒
打 燈 花 兒
爺 爺 兒 尋 了 個 禿 奶 奶 兒
眼 又 斜
嘴 又 歪
氣 的 爺 爺 兒 竟 發 獃

NOTES

剔 燈 棍 兒 t'i teng¹ kun¹ 'r, a wire to pull up the wick in an oil lamp. 打 燈 花 兒 ta³ teng¹ hua¹ 'r, to take away the burned part of the wick. — The scene depicted is rather a comic one; a man has married a woman whom he has never seen, and as soon as he enters the nuptial room, he snuffs the candle to see better and perceives that the bride is a very ugly one. 爺 爺 兒 ye² ye² 'r, means in vulgar Pekinese a man, a husband as 奶 奶 兒 nai³ nai³ 'r, means a woman, a wife. Both words are used in different meanings in family relations technology. 發 獃 fa¹ tai¹, to stare vacantly.

TRANSLATION

With the oil-lamp wire — he takes away the burned wick — the man perceives he has got for

himself a bald wife — she is squint eyed — and has
a crooked mouth — the husband is so struck with
anger — that he stares stupidity.

XVII

孃孃地進了房　香香
香香　地　香香
嚷掃走　兒兒　長掃香
姐郎帳子頭開來娘　香花瓣褥地來花
的帳床枕被子姑　鬧來娘　香簪花紅落兒合
的的的的海的鏡花玉桃大拖花百尖圓
兒兒兒兒兒菊兒花桂粉唇件裙蘂起兒兒
花花花花花秋人銀頭官朱一羅蘂掃蕖蕖
石莱芙繡蘭为綉虞兩梳臉嘴身下叫松芙荷
榴莉蓉花芝藥球美對油擦點绛地了花姑花

靈 芝 開 花 兒 抱 牡 丹
水 仙 開 花 兒 香 十 里
梔 子 開 花 兒 嫂 嫂 望 江 南

NOTES

It appears this song has no other aim than to put together the greatest number of flowers and plants names. 石 榴 花 shih² liu² hua¹, pomegranate flowers. 茉 莉 花 muo⁴ li⁴ hua¹, Arabian jasmine (lat. *Jasminum Sambœ*). 芙 蓉 花 fu¹ jung² hua¹, the Hibiscus mutabilis. 繡 花 hsiou⁴ hua¹, flowers embroidered by hand. 蘭 芝 花 lan² chih¹ hua¹, and also 蘭 花 lan² hua¹, the Cymbidium ensifolium. 繡 球 花 hsiou⁴ ch'iu¹ hua¹, sort of geranium (lat. *geranium zonale*). 鬧 嚷 嚷 nao⁴ jang¹ jang¹, to be noisy, here perhaps to be in confusion, to be meddled together. 秋 菊 ch'iu¹ chü², autumn chrysanthemum. 海 棠 hai³ t'ang², pyrus spectabilis, cultivated for its flowers and fruits. 虞 美 人 yü² mei² jen², papaver rhoeas, a double variety of the poppy. 桂 花 kuai⁴ hua¹, the Cassia flower (lat. *Cinnamomum Cassia*). 官 粉 kuan¹ fen³, sort of good white cosmetic powder which ladies rub on their cheeks 玉 簪 花 yü⁴ tsan¹ hua¹, Funkia subcordata. 下 地 hsia⁴-ti⁴, to reach the ground. 羅 裙 luo² ch'ün², a long petticoat, made with a sort of silk called 羅 luo². 拖 落 t'uo¹ lo⁴, is said of the dresses when they are too long and the skirts sweep the ground. 松 花 sung¹ hua¹, pincflower. The Chinese use to throw the flowers into the stove to prevent the bad smell of coal. 百合花 pae¹-ho²-hua¹ read also puo¹-ho²-hua¹, the lily (lat. *Lilium*). 茨姑 tz'u² ku¹, an herb with arrowlike leaves (lat. *Sagittaria sagittifolia*). 荷花 ho² hua¹, the Lotus blossom, the same as 蓮花 lien² hua¹, (lat. *Nelumbium speciosum*). 靈芝 ling² chih¹, the plant of long life. 水仙 shuei³ hsien¹, the narcissus. 栀子 chih¹-tzü, the gardenia 望江南 uang⁴ chiang¹ nan², means literally " looking towards the South of the river " but it is also a flower name.

TRANSLATION

The bride, is the pomegranate flower — the bridegroom is the jasmin — the curtains are covered with flowers of the Hibiscus mutabilis — the bed is covered with embroidered flowers — the pillow is covered with flowers of Cymbidium ensifolium — and the coverlet is spread with peony flowers — the mattress is strown w'th geraniums flowers, which are in disorder — they call the autumn chrysanthemum and the flower of the pyrus spectabilis, to let them sweep the floor — here miss poppy has entered the room — there are two mirrors with frames inlaid with silver — and she combs her hair as perfumed as the Cassia flower — then she rubs her face with white cosmetic powder, with the smell of the Funkia subcordata — and she marks a red spot on her lips, as scented as petals of the peach blossom —

she wears a big red overcoat — and a petticoat so
long that it sweeps the ground — then she calls the
pine flower that it may sweep the floor — the pine
flowers beegins to sweep the floor and a lily odour is
smelt — the leaves of the Sagittaria sagittifolia are
pointed — the leaves of the lotus blossom are round
— the plant of immortality opening the flowers
embraces the tree peony — the narcissus opens the
flowers and the odour is smelt as far as ten li — the
gardenia opens the flowers and the sister-in-law
"looks toward South."

XVIII

槐樹槐
槐樹底下搭戲台
人家的姑娘都來了
我家的姑娘還不來
說着說着就來了
騎着驢
打着傘
光着脊梁挽着纂

NOTES

槐樹 huai² shu⁴, the ash tree (lat. *fraxinus*). 打
着傘 ta³ cho¹ san³, keeping the umbrella open. 光
着脊梁 kuang¹ cho¹ chi³ niang³, bare from head to

waist. 挽着纂 uan³ cho¹ tsuan³, with the back-hair combed as a chignon.

TRANSLATION

Ash trees, ash trees — under the ash trees they have raised a stage — everybody's girls are come — only mine does not come yet — just while speaking, here she is come — riding on a donkey — with an open parasol — and with her hair combed into a chignon.

XIX

哥兒多飯
吃完了
打老婆
老婆上窗戶兒
打的窗戶沒有檔兒
打窗戶
窗戶照鏡兒
打的鏡子沒有底兒
打鏡子
鏡子唱曲兒
打的曲兒沒有頭兒
打曲兒
曲兒要猴兒
打的猴兒沒有圈兒
打猴兒
猴兒鑽天兒
打的老婆
二飯完了
小吃吃

There is not much coherence in the words, and the fun is in the fact that many verses are ended with the final 兒, which produces a ridiculous effect. 二 哥 eur⁴ ko¹, the second brother in the family also simply a familiar name. 老 婆 lao³ p'uo², an old woman, a wife. The accent falls generally on the 老 lao³ in this meaning ; but if said lao³ p'uo² tzŭ³, with the accent on the p'uo², then it means "a female servant". 檔 兒 tang⁴ 'r, small wood bars placed horizontally in the chinese window-sash. 耍 猴 兒 shua³ hou² 'r, " to (let) play the monkey, that is to exhibit the tricks of a monkey to gain the life "; the other metaphorical meaning is " to lark, to romp, to be impertinent". 圈 兒 ch'iuan¹ 'r, a wooden circle through which the monkeys are let jump.

TRANSLATION

The small second brother — eats too much — and when he has finished eating — he beats his wife — and the wife is so beaten that she jumps on the window — the window has no bars — and the wife is so beaten that she looks in the mirror — the mirror has no bottom — the wife is beaten so that she begins to sing — the song has no end — the wife is so beaten that she " plays with the monkey " —

the monkey has no circle — and the wife is so beaten that she springs up to the sky.

XX

金 軲 轆 棒
銀 軲 轆 棒
爺 爺 兒 打 板 兒
奶 奶 兒 唱
一 唱 唱 到 大 天 亮
養 活 了 個 孩 子 沒 處 兒 放
一 放 放 在 鍋 台 上
嗞 兒 嗞 兒 的 喝 米 湯

NOTES

軲轆棒 ku¹ lu¹ pang¹, a child toy, consisting in a short wood mace with a handle. The wood above the handle is circularly worked as to give the idea of wheels 軲 轆 ku¹ lu¹. It is the imitation of an ancient chinese weapon. 大天亮 ta¹ t'ien¹ liang¹, when the daylight was very bright. 嗞兒嗞兒 tzŭ¹ 'r tzŭ¹ 'r, imitates the sound produced by the lips of a person who is sipping broth. There was no character in the dictionary for it, but I was forced to adopt the above written as corresponding to the exact sound and having by side the radical 口.

Gilt wood mace — silvered wood mace — the husband strikes the castanets and the wife sings — and they have been singing till broad daylight — and she has born a child, and there was no place to lay him — and they have laid him on the kitchen-stove — where he is sipping the rice gravy.

XXI

```
批 批
批 䖱 輥 圓
家 家 門 前 掛 紅 線
紅 線 厚
甩 大 袖
一 甩 甩 在 門 後 頭
門 後 頭 刀
掛 腰 刀 尖
腰 刀 大 天
頂 大 打 雷
天 打 咬 賊
狗 咬 嚕 嘩
唷 嚕 嘩 拉 又 一 回
```

NOTES

These words are sung by children as they give each other the hand and turn around in a circle: no particulary defined meaning is attached to them, as they are put together only to keep measure with the steps. 轱轆圓 ku¹ lu⁴ yüan², as round as a wheel. 甩 shuai³, expresses a movement peculiar to the Chinese, that of letting down with a sudden jerk of the arm, the long sleeve which was tucked up the wrist. 唏嚕嘩拉 hsi¹ liu¹ hua¹ la¹, words with no meaning.

TRANSLATION

Draw, draw — draw the circle as round as a wheel — at every house-door is hanging a red thread — the red thread is thick — drop the sleeve — drop it as far as behind the door — behing the door — is hanging the swoard — the swoard is cutting — and is so long that it touches the sky — the sky thunders — the dog bites the thieves — hsiliuhualà once more !

XXII

大 秃 子 得 病
二 秃 子 慌

三 禿 子 請 大 夫
四 禿 子 熬 薑 湯
五 禿 子 抬
六 禿 子 埋
七 禿 子 哭 着 走 進 來
八 禿 子 問 他 哭 甚 麼
我 家 死 了 個 禿 乖 乖
快 快 兒 抬
快 快 兒 埋
別 讓 那 個 葫 蘆 子 兒 迸 出 來

NOTES

For a baldhead is meant in this song a child, for the reason explained before. 薑湯 chiang¹ t'ang¹, ginger broth, a medicine given to make the patient sweat. 乖乖 kuai¹ kuai¹, dear, treasure, said of children. 葫蘆子兒 hu² lu² tzŭ³ 'r, the seeds in his gourd (meaning his head). 迸出來 peng¹ ch'u¹ lai², to spring up; said of things which being thrown down, by force of elasticity, spring up.

TRANSLATION

The first baldhead gets sick — the second baldhead is scared — the third baldhead goes to call a doctor — the fourth baldhead boils a ginger decoction — the fifth baldhead bears him (the sick one) on the shoulders — the sixth baldhead buries him — the seventh baldhead comes in — the eight baldead asks "why do you weep"? — In my family a dear baldhead is dead — quickly take him away — quickly bury him — lest the seeds should spring out of his gourd.

XXIII

樹柴青
呀呀兒英
我跟姐姐過一冬
姐姐蓋着花花被褥
妹妹蓋着羊皮子襖
姐姐穿着紬子襖
妹妹穿着破皮襖
姐姐戴着金簪子
妹妹戴着竹圈子
姐姐騎着高頭馬
妹妹騎着樹喀杈
姐姐登着銀鐙兒
妹妹登着牆縫兒
姐姐抱着個銀娃娃
妹妹抱着個癩蛤蟆
走一步來哇兒呱哇兒呱又哇兒呱

NOTES

呀 呀 兒 英 ya¹ ya¹ 'r ying¹, meaningless refrain which rhymes with the preceding verse. 花 花 被 hua¹ hua¹ pei⁴, a coverlet embroidered with flowers. 簪 子, tsan¹ tzŭ, chinese hair-pin. 竹 圈 子 chu² ch'iüan¹ tzŭ, ear-rings made of bamboo; in Peking ear-rings are generally called 鉗 子 ch'ien² tzŭ. 嘠 杈 k'a¹ ch'a¹, a forked branch 癩 蛤 蟆 lai⁴ ha² ma¹, a scabby toad. 哇 兒 呱 ku¹ 'r kuà¹, imitates the voice of a toad.

TRANSLATION

The tree leaves are dark — I spend a winter with my elder sister — my elder sister covers her bed with a coverlet embroidered with flowers — and I the younger sister cover my bed with a goat skin — my elder sister wears a satin overcoat — I the younger sister wear a broken skin overcoat — my elder sister wears golden hair-pins — and I the younger sister wear bamboo ear-rings — my elder sister rides on a splendid horse — and I the younger sister ride on a forked branch — my elder sister leans her feet on silver stirrups — and I the younger sister lean my feet on the wall crevices — my elder sister holds in her arms a silver baby — and I the younger sister hold in my arms a scabby toad — which moves a step and then cries kurkuà kurkuà.

XXIV

立了秋來立了秋
八月十五月兒照高樓
鴉雀無聲人烟靜
賺見了兩個押虎子走籌
一根燈草嬾他不亮
兩根燈草又怕費了油
有心要買一枝羊油燭
怎奈我手中沒有猴兒頭

NOTES

立秋 li⁴ ch'iu¹, the beginning of winter. 照 chao⁴, illumines. 人烟靜, jen² yen¹ ching⁴, men and smoke (houses) are resting; everything is quiet. 押虎子 ya¹ hu³ tzŭ, Peking street watchmen, kept by the Government to tell the hour by striking on a bamboo rattle. 走籌 tsou³ ch'ou², to take round by night time a bamboo tally from one watch-post to another. 一根燈草 i¹ ken¹ teng¹ ts'ao³, a lamp wick made of the stalk of the Juncus communis (rushes). 怎奈 tsen³ nai⁴, there is no remedy, no way. 猴兒頭 'hou² 'r t'ou², a monkey's head, slang Pekinese term to mean money. Several words are used in the same meaning as for instance 大軲轆 ta⁴ ku¹ lu⁴, the big wheel. 官板 kuan¹ pan³, official stamp, stamped by the Government. Several terms cannot be written at all, wanting a character for them, not with standing I will venture to write them down with homophonous characters. So for instance 嘎, read ka². Ex. 我的這個褡連兒就剩了叫喚嘎了 uo³ ti¹ che¹-ko⁴ ta¹-lien² 'r ciou⁴ sheng⁴ la chiao⁴ huan⁴ ka² la, "there is noting left in my purse but noisy cash" meaning that the purse only contains two or three cash which at every step meet and ring. It is also said 古嘎 ku³ ka². Ex. 古嘎沒有 ku³ ka² mei² iou³, I have no cash. Another term is 側 ts'o², or 側羅 ts'o² lo². Foreign words are sometimes used as chi¹-ha¹, the chinese transformation of the Manchu word *jiha* " money" and chao¹ su¹, said to be Mongol and generally used, peculiarly in the whole phrase chao¹ su¹ u⁴ kuei³, which is meant for "I have no money" and is all in Mongol.

TRANSLATION

The autumn has set in, the autumn has set in — on the fifteenth of the eighth month the moon illumines the high palaces — crows and other birds are silent and men and houses are resting — I have seen two watchmen who went round taking the watch-tally — here, with only one wick in the lamp, I am sorry it is dark — but I am afraid to consume too much oil burning two wicks — I intend buying a candle of mutton-tallow — but, alas! I have not a single cash in the hands.

XXV

高樹稍軟翻了氣出眼戲

上柳兒兒潤唱子戲

糖兒愛到枝五直子戲

兒兒氷豆兒爬稍小兒髟了湯涼小

五六塊包五爬樹的六上完熱不的

小小一一小一柳挵小戴唱唱湯燙

小六兒叫親娘

NOTES

Chinese children are given by their parents a 奶名 nai³ ming³, "milk-name" by which they are designated in the family. These milk names are numberless. A common habit in the family is to give the new born children only a number for milk name, by which number the child is called *four* or *five,* if it is the fourth or fifth son in the family. The common forms for these arithmetical names are such: A first born may be called 一子 i¹-tzŭ, (the form is not much used; the accent falls on the i¹). The second son may be called 二哥 eur¹ ko¹, or 小一兒 hsiao³ i¹ 'r. The third son may be called 三兒 san¹ 'r, the fourth 四兒 ssŭ⁴ '-, the fifth 五兒 u³ 'r, the sixth 六兒 liou¹ 'r, and so forth as far as ten. These milk names are also given to children independently of their order in the family and become like our christian names Charles, John and so forth. 氷糖 ping¹ t'ang², white sugar in pieces sold on the streets to children. 一包豆兒 i¹ pao¹ tou¹ 'r, a parcel of roasted beans, another delicacy for children. 翻眼 fan¹ yen³, to turn up the eyes, like a man who loses his senses and shows the white of his eyes. 淘氣 t'ao²-ch'i¹, impertinent, saucy. 戴上鬍子 tai¹ shang¹ hu² tzŭ, to put on a false beard as actors do in theaters.

TRANSLATION

The small Five — and the small Six — with a piece of white sugar — and a parcel of beans — the small Five likes to go high up — and he climbs up to the tip of the branch of the willow tree — the tip of the willow branch is weak — and the small Five tumbles down and hurts himself so that he shows the white of his eyes. — The small Six is really impertinent — he puts on a false beard and sings an act of an opera — when he has finished singing the opera, — he drinks hot broth — the broth is not cool — and the small Six scalds himself so that he calls for his mother.

XXVI

小 小 子 兒
坐 門 礅 兒
哭 着 喊 着 要 媳 婦 兒
要 了 媳 婦 兒 作 甚 麼
點 上 燈 說 話 兒
吹 了 燈 作 伴 兒
明 兒 個 起 來 梳 小 辮 兒

NOTES

門礅兒 men³ tun¹ 'r, a big stone-seat placed by the side of a street door. 喊着 han³ cho, crying loudly.

TRANSLATION

The small boy — is sitting outside the door on the stone-seat — and weeping and wailing he wants to have a wife — when he has got a wife what will he do with her? — when the lamp is lighted he will have a chat with her — when then the lamp is out he will keep company with her —

and the next morning after getting up she will comb his small pigtail.

XXVII

高 高 山 上 有 一 家
十 間 房 子 九 間 塌
老 頭 子 出 來 拄 拐 棍 兒
老 婆 子 出 來 就 地 兒 擦
看 家 的 狗 兒 三 條 腿
避 鼠 的 貍 貓 短 個 尾 巴

NOTES

拄 chu⁷, to lean on a stick. 拐棍兒 kuai³ kun¹ 'r, a stick used by old men to lean on. 就地兒 chiou¹ ti¹ 'r, bent to the ground (walking) as very old men do. 擦 ts'a¹, to walk painfully dragging (rubbing) the feet on the ground. 避鼠的貓 pi¹ shu³ ti¹-mao¹, a cat which shuns (does not catch) mice. 貍貓 li² mao¹, the wild cat.

TRANSLATION

On a very high mountain there lives a family — of the ten rooms in the building nine rooms are in ruin — the old man goes out leaning on a stick —

and the old wife walks painfully and bent to the ground. — the dog which watches the house has only three legs — the wild cat which does not catch the mice is without a tail.

XXVIII

香 香 蒿 子
刺 刺 罐 兒
苦 麻 兒
香 荽 兒
喇 叭 喇 叭 花 兒
翠 雀 兒
買 我 的 是 好 漢 兒
買 別 人 的 是 龜 蓋 兒 喲

NOTES

These words are sung by Pekinese boys who want to imitate the ambulant grocer, and tell aloud the names of their wares. 香蒿子 hsiang¹ hao¹ tzŭ, the Artemisia annua-the chinese make with its dry stalks a sort of vegetable rope which they burn to keep away mosquitoes. 刺刺罐兒 la¹ la¹ kuan⁴ ’r, a wild grass which grows at the beginning of spring. 苦蕒兒 or 苦菜 k’u³ ts’ai⁴, the sowthistle (lat. *Lonchus arvensis*). 香荽 hsiang¹ ts’ai⁴, “odorous herbs” (lat. *Coriandrum sativum*) the chinese use its leaves for parsley. 喇叭花 la³ pa¹ hua¹, "trumpet flowers" is the white stramony (lat. *Datura alba*). 翠雀兒 ts'uei¹ ch'iao³ 'r, the larkspur (lat. *Delfinium anthriscifolium*). 龜蓋兒 kuei¹ kai⁴ 'r, a mild form of the common chinese insult "turtle-shell".

TRANSLATION

Here is Artemisia annua — here is lalaqua'r grass — here are sowthistle and parsley — white stramony flowers — and larkspur — who buys my ware is a good fellow — and who buys other people's is a "turtle-shell".

XXIX

泥 泥 泥 泥 餑 餑
泥 泥 泥 泥 人 兒
老 頭 兒 喝 酒 不 讓 人 兒
買 我 的 是 個 好 漢 兒
不 買 我 的 是 個 王 八 蛋 兒

NOTES

Chinese boys are till a certain age as busy in the manufacture of mud-pies as any other boy in foreign countries. They buy for a few cash ready-made moulds out of which they work pagodas,

small fishes, turtles, and so forth. When the wares
are ready and dry, the small merchants sing these
verses as if they meant to sell the products of their
work. 泥餑餑 ni² puo¹ puo¹, is the exact equivalent
of the english "mud-pie".

TRANSLATION

Here are mud pies — here are mud figures —
the old man drinks wine and does not offer to
others — who buys my ware is a good fellow — and
who does not buy mine is a turtle's egg.

XXX

水 牛 兒 水 牛 兒
先 出 觭 角 後 出 頭
你 爹 你 媽
給 你 買 下 燒 肝 兒 燒 羊 肉

NOTES

In all countries children have verses to address
snails, and in China too, although the meaning of
the verses is not to be looked for. 水牛兒 shuei³
niu² 'r, the snail.

TRANSLATION

Snail, snail — you first show out your horns and

then your head — your father and mother — will
buy for you some roasted liver and roasted mutton.

XXXI

麩段條來肉六腿不黎糕脆個豆西辣兒白五塊兒

吃老細兒吃老後瘦吃糖真一喝老的菜吃老大味

要找兒棍要找兒瘦要冰呀的要找瓜要找兒的

兒你條子兒你窩肥兒酥大兒得酸黃兒你穰子

妞給寬簾妞給腰真妞還真好妞還酸酸妞給黃栗

兒不哼哎喲
兒哼哎喲
塊兒汁兒呀兒呀哼哎喲
的兒不哼哎喲
兒呀哼哎喲

NOTES

妞兒 niu¹ 'r, girl, familiar term for 姑娘 ku¹ niang². 吃麪 ch'ih¹ mien⁴, to eat vermicelli. 麪 mien⁴ is here for 麪條兒 mien⁴ t'iao² 'r, 老叚 Laŏ³ tuan⁴, the old man named Tuan, probably a shop-keeper. 寬條兒 k'uan¹ t'iao² 'r, flat and large vermicelli. 細條兒 hsi⁴ t'iao² 'r, finer vermicelli. 簾子棍兒 lien²-tzŭ³ kun⁴ 'r, another sort of vermicelli so called because of its resemblance to the bamboo sticks which are bound together to form a summer curtain. 來不哼哎喲 lai² pu eng a-yo, meaningless refrain. 腰窩兒 iao¹ uo¹ 'r, "the loins nest" the best part of the loins of a mutton or a beef. 後腿兒 hou⁴ t'uei³ 'r, the back part of the thigh. 眞肥瘦 chen¹ fei² shou⁴, " really there are both fat and lean", that is very good meat-a buyer going to the butcher's shop, if not particularly wishing to get more fat or more lean, calls the meat he wants 肥瘦 fei² shou⁴ that is fat and lean together. So the phrase 你給我一斤肥瘦兒 ni³ kei³ uo³ i¹ chin¹ fei² shou⁴ 'r, means " give me a pound of good meat". 棃糕 li² kao¹, pear jam dried in slices. 酥 su¹, is said of the food and particularly of pastry, when it is so delicate that it melts in the mouth-french " fondant". 脆 ts'uei⁴, crisp. 豆汁兒 tou⁴ chih¹ 'r, a decoction of seeds which is drunk in spring time and is thought a powerful agent to cool one's blood : it is mostly used by Bannermen. 老西兒 lao³ hsi¹ 'r, nickname given

by the Pekinese to the natives of the Shan-hsi
province, who do not enjoy a very good reputation,
even among Pekinese. Here they are quoted
because they are generally fond of sour food as
the tou¹-chih¹ is. 黄 瓜 菜 huang² kua¹ ts'ai¹, salted
cucumber. 白 薯 pae² shu³, the sweet potatoes. 瓤
兒 jang² 'r, the pulp of a fruit, the stuff of a pudding,
generally the interior of objects, from a cake to a
clock.

TRANSLATION

Young lady, if you want to eat vermicelli, — we
will go to see the old Tuan for you, — who has flat
vermicelli, and thin vermicelli — and "curtain-
sticks" vermicelli — Young lady, if you want to eat
meat — we will go to the old Six's for you — he
has got good loin of mutton and good haunch of
mutton — both fat and lean meat — Young lady, if
you want to eat pear-jam — we must also boil it in
white sugar — it is really melting in the mouth and
so crisp! — and what a big slice of it! — Young
lady, if you want to drink bean decoction — then
we must go to the old Shan-hsi man's — how sour it
is! how bitter it is! — and how sour the salt
cucumbers taken with it — Young lady, if you want
to eat sweet potatoes — we will go to the old
Five's — who has there large slices of sweet potato
pulp — which smell like chestnuts.

XXXII

出了門兒
陰了天兒
抱着肩兒
進茶館兒
靠爐台兒
找個朋友兒　尋倆錢兒
出茶館兒
飛雪花兒
老天爺
竟和窮人鬧着頑兒

NOTES

These verses are supposed to be uttered by a beggar who complains of his bad luck on a winter's day. The song is rhymed by adding the character 兒 eur² at the end of each verse. 抱着肩兒 pao¹ cho² chien¹ 'r, lit. "embracing one's shoulder" that is to keep the arms folded on the breast, as chinese beggars do when they feel cold. 爐台兒 lu² t'ai² 'r, a small stove made of bricks. 尋 hsin², means to ask something from somebody, to look for, the ordinary sound of the character is hsün. 老天爺 lao³ t'ien¹ ye², the old gentleman in the sky. Has no relation whatever with our religious beliefs. — the expression is a very common one but the same Chinese are the first to be puzzled when asked for the meaning. It is a personification of the providence, luck, justice, and also weather, and is as undefined a word as many others in Chinese. 雪花兒 hsüe³ hua¹ 'r, lit. snow-flowers, snow-flakes. 鬧着頑兒 nao⁴ cho² uan² 'r, to play with, to make sport with.

TRANSLATION.

As soon I have gone out — the weather has become cloudy — folding my arms on my breast — I enter a tea-shop — I lean against the brick stove — and look for a friend from whom I may beg some money — as I go out of the tea-shop — here snow-flakes are falling — the old gentleman in the sky — only likes to make sport with us poor people.

XXIII

搭連兒搭
我和褡連兒作親家
親家的姑娘會梳頭
一梳梳了個麵子熟
麥子磨成麵油
芝蔴磨成油架
黃瓜上了架溜
茄子打提溜

NOTES

The beginning of the song does not seem to have any comprehensible meaning and I can only translate it literally. 褡連兒 ta¹ lien² 'r, cloth purse in which the chinese keep their banknotes, called also 錢褡連兒 ch'ien² ta¹ lien¹ 'r, money purse. Another sort is styled 檳榔褡連兒 ping¹ lang² ta¹ lien² 'r, and is used for holding betel nuts, as the name shows. 作親家 tsuo⁴ ch'in¹ chia¹, to become a relative. The word ch'in¹ chia¹ means all relations who bear a different family name. The word is in modern Pekinese wrongly pronounced ch'ing⁴ chia¹. 梳了個麥子熟 shu¹ la¹ ko⁴ mai⁴ tzŭ shou², she has taken as much time to comb her hair, as would be required for the wheat to become ripe in the fields. 上了架 "has grown on the bower". Cucumber plants are made creep on small bowers. 打提溜 ta³ ti¹ liu¹, to swing, pushed by the wind.

TRANSLATION

The purse, the purse — I have become a relation of the purse — the purse family's girl knows how to dress her hair — and has taken as much time to comb it as is required for the wheat to get ripe — for the wheat to be ground and made into flour — for the sesamum to be ground and made into ail — for the cucumber to grow on the bowers — and for the brinjal fruit to be swung by the wind.

XXXIV

羅鍋子橋
一磴兒到比一磴兒高
燈籠兒鬧草水皮兒漂
金魚兒咬着銀魚尾兒
大肚子的蝦蟆
哇兒呱哇兒呱的叫

NOTES

This stanza is composed in praise of the fine scenery in the Emperor's Summer palace grounds, where the hunchbacked bridge is also to be seen. 一磴兒 i[1] teng[4] 'r, a step in a staircase, in a flight of stairs. 鬧草 cha[2] ts'ao[3], grass wich grows near the gatelocks, called also 燈籠兒草 teng[1] lung[2] 'r ts'ao[3], "lantern grass" from its leaves being strung to a stalk like so many chinese lanterns to a rope. 金魚兒 chin[1] yü[2] 'r, "goldfish". 水皮兒 shuei[3] p'i[2] 'r, the surface of the water, lit. "the water skin". 銀魚兒 yin[2] yü[2] 'r, "silverfish".

TRANSLATION

On the hunchback bridge — one step is higher than the other — under the bridge the leaves of the lantern grass float on the water — the goldfish

run after the silverfish and bite their tails — and
the toads with big bellies — cry kurkuà kurkuà.

XXXV

東 嶽 廟
東 廊 下
東 廊 下 有 個 墪 兒
蹲 着 個 金 眼 綠 毛 龜 兒
解 南 來 了 個 鬼 兒
桃 着 一 担 水 兒
搁 下 水 兒 撿 根 棍 兒
單 打 金 眼 綠 毛 龜 兒 的 腿 兒

NOTES

東嶽 tung¹ yü⁴, one of the five sacred mountains,
the 泰山 t'ai⁴ shan¹, in the Shantung province. 墪
兒 tun¹ 'r, a small earth moud. Each verse ends with
the character 兒 eur², which gives fun to the song.

TRANSLATION

In the temple of mount T'ai-shan — under the
east verandah — under the east verandah there
is an earth mound — on which squats a turtle with
golden eyes and a shell covered with green moss
— from the south has come a devil — bearing on his

shoulders a load of water — he lays down the water, picks up a stick — and only strikes the legs of the turtle with golden eyes and the shell covered with moss.

XXXVI

大 娘 子 喝 酒
二 娘 子 筵
三 娘 子 捧 過 小 菜 碟 兒 來
四 娘 子 來 回 的 去 端 菜
五 娘 子 一 傍 把 座 兒 安 排
他 說 是 大 家 湊 個 團 圓 會
消 拳 行 令 樂 開 懷

NOTES

大 娘 子 ta⁴ niang² tzŭ, is the wife of the first brother in the family. 二 娘 子 eur⁴ niang² tzŭ, is the wife of the second brother and so forth. 篩 酒 shai¹ chiou³, to warm the wine before drinking it. 捧 p'eng³, to keep on one's hands, to present, to offer. 小 菜 兒 hsiao³ ts'ai⁴ 'r, salted vegetables with which the Chinese relish their food. 端 菜 tuan¹ ts'ai⁴, to bring the food on the table. — 傍 i p'ang², by the side, aside. 團 圓 會 t'uan² yüan² huei⁴, general feast in which all the members of the family collect to dine together. This day falls on the fifteenth of the eighth month, because in that night the moon is perfectly full 團 圓 t'uan² yüan². 樺 拳 hua² ch'iüan², to play at guessfingers, at morra. 行 令 hsing² ling¹, literary amusement. Somebody in the company begins by giving a verse or a classical phrase, and the other members of society must follow by inventing another verse or phrase with the same rhyme, or with the same parallelism of words, or the same style of allusions. The man who first exhausts his stock of phrases is punished by being forced to drink a number of glasses of wine.

TRANSLATION

The first lady drinks w'ne — the second lady warms the wine — the third ladies come bringing in small saucers with salted cucumbers — the fourth lady at the side arranges the places (covers) — she says that every body has come for a complete meeting — to play at guessfingers, to play at allusions game, and to be merry.

XXXVII

禿 子 禿　　　籠 出 油 來
上 腦 籠　　　煎 豆 腐

NOTES

These words are sung to tease the boys, who

have their hair shaven. 箍 ku¹, a whoop, an iron belt put about barrels. 腦箍 nao³ ku¹, is the name of an old instrument of torture consisting of a red hot circle of iron which was put on the head.

TRANSLATION

You baldhead — we will put a red hot whoop round your head — and with the oil we will press out of it — we will fry bean-cake.

XXXVIII

蒤 連 兒 搭
我 和 裕 連 兒 作 親 家
親 家 的 姑 娘 病 兒 沉 診
請 了 個 大 夫 把 胍 診
開 了 個 藥 方 兒 把 藥 尋
開 的 是 蚊 子 膯
蚯 蚤 心
蒼 蠅 翅 膀 兒 要 半 斤

NOTES

The beginnig of this song is identical with that of song N⁰ 33. 診胍 chen¹ muo¹, to feel the pulse as chinese doctors do. 藥方 iao¹ fang medical prescription written and signed by the physician.

蚊子 uen² tzu, the mosquito.　蛤蚤 ko⁴ tsao³, the flea.
蒼蠅 ts'ang¹ ying², the fly.

TRANSLATION

The purse, the purse — I am now a relation of the purse family — but their daughter has grown dangerously sick — and they have called a physician who has felt her pulse — and then has written a prescription, and people have gone to buy the medicines — on the prescription there is written: mosquito's livers, flea's hearts and half a pound of flies wings.

XXXIX

三 兒 三 兒
穿 的 是 甚 撒 兒
穿 的 是 青 洋 縐 褲 子
青 洋 縐 汗 褡 兒
梳 着 個 牛 糞 狐 兒
左 邊 戴 着 晚 香 玉
右 邊 戴 着 茉 莉 花 兒
五 分 底 兒 的 雙 臉 兒 鞋
漂 白 的 襪 子 明 期 臉 兒

NOTES

These words are addressed to a young girl, as

may be seen from the description of her dress, which follows. The slang word sa² 'r, not generally known even among Pekinese, means dress, fashion, toilette. As no written character exists to represent this sound and this meaning, I have used for it the character sa 撒 which being originally in the first tone, here ought to be read in the second. Wanting to find a character for the word, it could be formed this combination 薂 to be read sa² 'r. — One of the phrases commonly heard is this 你有撒兒沒撒兒 ni³ iou³ sa² 'r, mei² sa² 'r? — meaning "have you got a good dress or not? 洋縐 yang² chou¹, crape imported by foreigners. 汗褟兒 han⁴ t'a¹ 'r, sort of cloth under-dress or shirt worn by Chinese in contact with the skin. European shirts are mostly styled 汗衫 han⁴ shan¹. 牛糞 niu² fen⁴ "ox-dung", name for a sort of head dress, more decently called 圓頭 yüan² t'ou² "round head". 觚 p'ai³, character not noted in the dictionaries but mentioned by Sir T. Wade in his Tone exercises. It means "to let onself down, to lie down, and then to be seated, placed". Here it is used as a noun, and is referred to the chignon placed on the girl's head. 晚香玉 uan³ hsiang¹ yü⁴, the gem which smells in the evening, the tuberosa (lat. *Polianthes tuberosa*). 五分底兒 u³-fen¹ ti³ 'r, thick five fen. The fen is the tenth part of the ts'un, an inch. The shoe sole is called 底兒 ti³ 'r, or 底子 ti³ tzu. and may be as thick as five or six inches. That sort of heel which is placed sometimes in the center of the sole in

ladies shoes is called 花 盆 底 兒 hua¹ p'en² ti³ 'r,
" flower-pot heel ". 雙 臉 兒 鞋 shuang¹ lien 'r hsie²,
literally " two faced shoes,, are so called when two
ornamental leather strings, come from. under the
sole on the point of the shoe. 漂 白 p'iao¹ pai²,
whitewashed, painted in white — the character 漂
is here vulgarly p'iao³. 明 期 臉 兒 ming² ch'i lien³ 'r,
chinese socks are so called when the seam is to be
seen in the middle.

TRANSLATION

San'r, San'r, what sort of dress have you put
on ? — " I have put on trowsers made of foreign
crape — and a shirt made of foreign crape — my
hair is combed in a round chignon — on the left of
it I have stuck a tuberose — and to the right a
jasmine — then I have got shoes with a sole half-
inch thick and with leather ornaments — and white
socks with the seam to be seen outside.

XL

哶 哶 羊   抓 把 草
跳 花 牆   餵 他 娘

NOTES

哶 mie¹, the sheep's bleating. 他 娘 t'a¹ niang²,
the small sheep's mother. This is one of those

little songs the mothers teach their children, when they begin to speak.

TRANSLATION

The bleating small sheep — has jumped over the flowery wall — to catch a bunch of grass — and to feed her mother.

XLI

大 翻 車
小 翻 車
一 翻 翻 了 個 花 大 姐
紅 袿 兒
綠 襖 兒
丁 香 小 脚 兒
對 面 喝 酒 兒
倒 像 親 姐 兒 倆

NOTES

The beginning of this song is not clear; it appears that the disposition of words in the first and in the second verse is irregular, saying 大翻車 小翻車 ta⁴ fan¹ tch'o¹-hsiao¹¹ fan ch'o instead of 大車翻 小車翻 ta⁴ ch'o¹ fan¹-hsiao³ ch'o¹ fan¹, meaning the big cart has overturned, the small cart has overturned. Furthermore the song speaks at the beginning of only one girl and it ends with two. That shows the song is not complete and every cart is supposed to be occupied by a girl. 花大姐 hua¹ ta¹ chie³, lit. "a flowery elder sister" means, a beautiful and well dressed girl. It is also said in the same sense 花妞兒 hua¹ niu¹ 'r. 丁香 ting hsiang, clove, very small feet are compared to grains of clove.

TRANSLATION

A big cart has overturned — a small cart has overturned — and a very beautiful young lady has fallen out of one — (and another young lady has fallen too) — with a red petticoat — and a green overcoat — with feet as small as grains of clove — they drink wine one in front of the other — and really are very much like two sisters.

XLII

高高山上一座小廟兒
裏頭坐着個神道兒
頭上戴頂羅帽兒
身上穿件外套兒
兩個小鬼喝道兒
四個小鬼抬着籐轎兒
出了門兒一遶兒
出巡回來歸廟兒

NOTES

神道 shen² tao⁴, a spirit. 外套兒 uai⁴ t'ao⁴ 'r, "external cover" is a sort of long dress, worn externally. 喝道兒 ho¹ tao⁴ 'r, and also 喝道子 ho¹ tao⁴ tzŭ, to shout before the chair of an official to make way. 籐轎 t'eng² chiao⁴, a light chair made of rattan. 一遶兒 i jao⁴ 'r, a turn, a stroll. 出巡 ch'u¹ hsün¹, to go out on a tour of inspection.

TRANSLATION

On a very high mountain there is a small temple — and inside sits a spirit — he wears on his head a crape-hat — and wears on his body a long gown — two small devils go in front shouting for room — four small devils bear the rattan-chair — he has gone out for a stroll — to make an inspection and then returning comes back to the temple.

XLIII

新打一把茶壺亮堂堂
新買一個小猪兒不吃糠
新娶一個媳婦兒不吃飯
眼淚汪汪想他親娘

NOTES

打 ta³, to beat, to strike, to work in metal. 亮

堂堂 liang¹ t'ang¹ t'ang¹, very bright; the character 堂 is originally read in the second tone, but here is pronounced in the first. 糠 k'ang¹, husks of grain with which pigs are fed.

TRANSLATION

A newly made metal tea-kettle is very bright — a newly bought small pig does not eat husks of grain — a newly married wife does not take food — she weeps profusely and thinks of her mother.

XLIV

一 進 門 兒 喜 冲 冲
院 子 裏 頭 搭 大 棚
洞 房 屋 子 把 燈 點
新 姑 娘 一 傍 淚 盈 盈
新 郎 不 住 的 來 回 觀
說 你 不 吃 點 兒 東 西 兒
我 可 心 疼

NOTES

This song contains a sketch of marriage ceremonies. 喜冲冲 hsi³ ch'ung¹ ch'ung¹ very merrily and with much noise. The character 冲 ch'ung means to shake, to dash against, but here it is only used to mean confusion, hurry, disorder. 洞房 tung⁴ fang², the bridal room. 淚盈盈 lei⁴ ying¹ ying, with many tears. 盈 盈 ying¹ ying, flowing, in great quantity, said of tears. The character 盈 is here in the first tone, but its regular tone is the second, and ought to be read ying². 新 郎 hsin¹ lang², the bridegroom. 不 住 的 pu⁴ chu⁴ ti, without interruption. 來 囘 lai² huei², repeatedly.

TRANSLATION

Entering the gate, how merry it is! — in the courtyard they have raised a big shed — in the bridal room the lamp is lighted — the bride in a corner is weeping bitterly — the bridegroom repeatedly calls to her — and says: if you do not take some food — my heart will ache.

XLV

和 尙 和 尙 搖 鈴 鐺
嘚 兒 嗒 喽 喝 我 騎 上
騎 到 那 兒 去
騎 到 天 邊 兒 去

NOTES

This song is repeated by boys to ridicule the buddhist priests who go round begging, and read their sacred books shaking a small bell. They are therefore compared to asses and mules which are similarly provided with bells. 鈴 鐺 ling² tang¹, a small bell — 且兒搭 pronounce törtà, a peculiar voice to get the mule, or the ass to walk. There are of course no characters for it and those written above not only are completely arbitrary, but do not exactly correspond to the pronunciation. The same is to be said for the word 倭喝 uo-ho, which has the same meaning.

TRANSLATION

Oh the bonze, the bonze is shaking the bell — go ahead! I will ride him — ride how far? — as far as the boundary of the sky.

XLVI

小 屄 屄 兒
怎 麼 那 麼 奸
四 兩 猪 肉 約 半 天
左 嫌 小 右 嫌 少
抱 着 猪 頭 往 家 跑

NOTES

These words are sung to insult Mohammedans who are not allowed to eat pork. 左 右 tsuo³ iuo⁴, right and left (the Chinese right hand being the European left hand). Means now and now, several times, repeatedly.

TRANSLATION

The small Mohammedan — how deceitful is he! — to buy only four ounces of pork, he is weighing for a good half-day — now he complains it is little and then he complains again it is little — then folding in his arms a pig's head he runs home.

XLVII

一呀二呀，
倒打連三棍兒，
花棍兒五，
銅錢數六，
鏨鏨兒七，
銀錠兒，
花花打打兩丈一，
兩甚麼兩，
二馬掌，
二甚麼二，
雙夾棍兒，
雙甚麼雙，
虎攢槍，
虎甚麼虎，
牛皮鼓，
牛甚麼牛，
磕郎毬，
磕甚麼磕，
燕于窩，
燕甚麼燕，
扯花線，
扯甚麼扯，
孫臏扯，
孫甚麼孫，
呂洞賓，
呂甚麼呂，
瘸柺兒李，
瘸甚麼瘸，
竈王爺，
竈甚麼竈，
城隍廟，
城甚麼城，

肚 兒 疼 　　　　雪 花 兒 飄

肚 甚 麼 肚 　　　雪 甚 麼 雪

搖 葫 蘆 　　　　孫 猴 兒 倒 打 猪 八 戒

搖 甚 麼 搖

NOTES

Chinese children practice a game which is also known by boys in foreign countries. Two boys sit one facing the other and strike first their own hands together and then each other's. To keep measure with the movement they mark, the time with these words, which are meaningless, and are huddled together only for the sake of the final rhymes. The game is called 打花巴掌 ta³ hua¹ pa¹ chang³. 呀 ya¹, is purely phonetic and meaningless. 倒打 tao⁴ ta³, to strike alternately — here the character 倒 is pronounced in the fourth and not in the third tone. 連三棍兒 lien² san¹ kun⁴ 'r, uninterruptedly three sticks (that is to say three blows). 數 in the third tone shu³, means to calculate, to reckon. 鏨 tsán, to carve, to chisel. 鏨子 tsan⁴ tzŭ, a chisel. 銀錠 yin² ting⁴, an ingot of silver. 夾棍兒 chia¹ kun⁴ 'r, an instrument of torture to squeeze the ankles lit. squeezing sticks. 嗑郎毬 k'o¹ lang¹ ch'iu²; I cannot find any explanation of this. The Chinese say that they do not know the meaning of the word. All that I could get from them is that the vulgar word k'o¹-lang 'r. means a corner, and is used instead of the more common 噶拉兒 ka¹-la² 'r (written according to Sir Thomas Wade's manner). The word ch'iu² is a ball. Could it be an "empty ball"? — 孫 臏 Sun¹-pin¹ a remarkable minister in the old state of Jen ; generally known by all children. 呂 洞 賓 Lü³ tung⁴ pin¹, one of the eight genii. 鐵 柺 李 t'ie³ kuai³ li³, another of the eight genii, a lame man called also: 瘸 柺 李 ch'üe² kuai³ li³, 竈 王 爺 tsao⁴ uang² ye², The god of the cooking stoves, familiar chinese god to whom a sacrifice is offered the 23ᵈ day of the twelfth moon. The god is said to have a wife called 竈 王 奶 奶 tsao⁴ uang² nai² nai³; she is worshipped in chinese families, but not in the shops, in which only the Tsao-uang is worshipped. 城 隍 廟 ch'eng² huang² miao⁴, the tutelar god of chinese cities. 搖 葫 蘆 iao² hu² lu², to shake a pumpkin, one of the favourite amusements of chinese babies, who are very often seen deeply absorbed in shaking a small calabash. 孫 猴 兒 sun¹ hou²'r, the monkey traveller in the novel 西 遊 記 Hsi¹-yu²-chi⁴, Re-collections of wanderings in the west countries. 猪 八 戒 chu¹ pa¹ chie⁴, a pig spoken of in the same novel as lazy and uxorious and therefore severely beaten by the monkey who was in charge of his education. These notions although taken from a novel in literary style, yet are generally known by the people, that have besides many ditties and rhymes on the subject.

TRANSLATION

One, two — let us strike alternately three

blows — five flowery sticks — count the cash — six chisels — seven ingots of silver — let us strike as long as two chang and one foot (!) — two, what two? — two horse shoes — two, what two? — a pair of squeezing sticks — a pair, what pair? — the tiger bears a gun on its shoulders — tiger, what tiger? — a drum covered with ox skin — ox, what ox? — an empty ball (?) — K'o[4], what K'o[4]? — a swallow's nest — swallow, what swallow? — pull the flowery thread — pull, what pull? — Sun pin pulls — Sun, what Sun? — Lü[3]·tung[4] pin — Lü[3], what Lü[3]? — The lame genius 'Ch'üe[2] kuai[3] 'r li[3] — Ch'üe[2], what ch'üe? — The god of the cooking stoves. — Stove, what stove? — The god protector of the city — City, what city? — The belly aches — belly, what belly? — shake the pumpkin — shake, what shake? — Snow-flakes are whirling round — snow, what snow? — The monkey Sun[1] Chu[1]-po[1]-chie[4],

XLVIII

打花巴掌的正月正
老太太愛逛個蓮花兒燈
燒着香兒念着佛兒
茉莉茉莉花兒串枝蓮
打花巴掌的二月二
老太太愛吃個白糖棍兒
燒着香兒念着佛兒

烟蓮　蓮薯　蓮肉　蓮鷄　鴨蓮　蓮

蓮枝三東兒枝四刺兒枝五白兒枝六煮兒枝七煮兒枝八燉兒枝九

串月關佛串月摘佛串月生佛串月白佛串月白佛串月白佛串月

兒三個着兒四不着兒五個着兒六個着兒七個着兒八個着兒九

花的吃念花的魚念花的吃念花的吃念花的吃念花的吃念花的

莉掌愛兒莉掌吃兒莉掌愛兒莉掌愛兒莉掌愛兒莉掌愛兒莉掌

茉巴太香茉巴太香茉巴太香茉巴太香茉巴太香茉巴

莉花太着莉花太着莉花太着莉花太着莉花太着莉花

茉打老燒茉打老燒茉打老燒茉打老燒茉打老燒茉打

老太太愛吃個白花藕
燒着香兒念着佛兒
茉莉茉莉花兒串枝蓮
打花巴掌的十月一
老太太愛吃個雪花梨
燒着香兒念着佛兒
茉莉茉莉花兒串枝蓮

NOTES

This song, like the last one is also sung by boys when playing at 打花巴掌 ta³ hua¹ pa¹ chang³. 正月正 cheng¹ yüe⁴ cheng¹, the first moon. 蓮花燈 lien² hua¹ teng¹, Lantern made of paper and shaped like a lotus flower. 逛燈 kuang⁴ teng¹, means to go out on the streets to look at the different shows of lanterns exhibited during five days, from the thirteenth to the seventeenth in the first month in the year. The regular day for the show is the 15th on which falls the 燈節 teng¹ chie² feast of lanterns. 念着佛 nien⁴ cho Fuo³, uttering prayers before Buddha. 串枝蓮 ch'uan⁴ chih¹ lien², a wild flower not unlike the lotus. This refrain is repeated at every couplet. We translate it only once. 白糖棍兒 pai² t'ang² kun⁴'r, small sugar sticks bought by children. 關京烟 kuan¹ tung¹ yen¹, toba co from Manchuria, the best quality of tobacco. 摘刺 chai² tz'u⁴, to take away the bones from a fish. 生白薯 sheng¹ pai² shu³, uncooked sweet potato. 燉鴨 tun⁴ ya¹, a stewed duck. 白花藕 pai² hua¹ ou³, a flour made from the root-stock of the lotus. 雪 花 棃 hsüe[3] hua[1] l[2], sort of very good pears found in Shantung, whose pulp is said to be as white as flakes of snow.

TRANSLATION

Strike the hands, in the first month of the year — the old lady likes to go out to look at the lotus-lanterns — burning incense and saying prayers — with jasmines, jasmines and wild lotus — Strike the hands, the second day of the second moon — the old lady likes to eat sugar sticks — Strike the hands, the third day of the third moon — the old lady likes to smoke Manchurian tobacco. Strike the hands, the fourth day of the fourth moon — the old lady likes to eat fish without taking the bones away. — Strike the hands, the fifth of the fifth moon — the old lady likes to eat raw yams — strike the hands, the sixth day of the sixth moon — the old lady likes to eat boiled pork — strike the hands, the seventh day of the seventh moon — the old lady likes to eat a boiled chicken with no sauce — strike the hands, the eighth day of the eighth moon — the old lady likes to eat stewed duck — strike the hands, the ninth day of the ninth moon — the old lady likes to eat lotus root flour — strike the hand, the first day of the tenth moon — the old lady likes to eat snow-white pears.

XLIX

打 羅 兒 篩
曳 羅 兒 篩
麥 子 熟 了 請 你 的 伯
你 伯 愛 吃 肉 兒 的
你 叔 愛 吃 豆 兒 的

NOTES

These words are not heard within the walls of Peking, but in the country. 羅兒 luo²'r a sift to *eve/* bolt flour. 曳 ye¹, to drag, to pull, to shake. 伯 read by the peasants not puo² but pai¹, one's father's elder brother. This character is read also pai³, in the word 大伯子 ta⁴ pai³ tzu, title given to a man by his younger brother's wife. 叔 shu² read here shou², as the peasants do. One's father's younger brother.

TRANSLATION

Beating the sieve sift! — shaking the sieve sift! — when the wheat is ripe, we will invite your uncle — your elder uncle likes to eat meat — your younger uncle likes to eat beans.

———————

L

一　副　筐
八　根　兒　繩
挑　起　了　阿　　扁　擔　遊　九　城
賣　蔥　阿　兒　阿
賣　蒜　兒　菜　兒
賣　青　菜　兒
打　鼓　兒
喝　雜　銀　錢　兒
唉　首　飾　來　賣

NOTES

These words are sung by children to imitate the perambulating vendors in the street. 一副筐 i¹ fu⁴ k'uang¹ a pair of baskets hanging from the pole called 扁擔 pien³ tan. 八根兒繩 pa¹ ken¹'r sheng², eight strings. As every basket is attached to an end of the pole by four strings, so eight strings comes to mean a porter's pole and more generally every sort of small chinese industry practiced by vendors furnished with such a pole. 九城 chiu³ ch'eng², the nine cities, the city of Peking. 青菜 ch'ing¹ ts'ai⁴ every sort of green vegetable. After speaking of the vendors of vegetables the song comes to speak of a curious sort of small industry practiced in Peking. Two men go together. One marches forward and beats a little drum, the other bearing

on the shoulder a pole with baskets calls loudly for
people who are willing to sell silver head-ornaments,
or other small objects of value.   This proceeding is
called 喝 雜 銀 錢 ho¹ tsa² yin² ch'ien², to call for different (and bad quality) silver to buy them for ready
money.

TRANSLATION

With a pair of baskets — are provided all the
small pedlars — with pole and baskets they go all
over the city — to sell onions — to sell garlic — to
sell green vegetables — the man who beats the
drum — and the other who cries: I buy objects
of silver — ohè, (who has got) head ornaments let
him come and sell.

LI

翻 餅 烙 餅
油 炸 餡 兒 餅
翻 過 來 瞧 瞧

NOTES

Chinese boys playing together take each other
by the hands and then turn round without separating
the hands.   The movement of turning round is
likened to the action of turning a pie on the pan,

and so this game is called 翻餅烙餅 fan¹ ping³ lao¹ ping³. 烙餅 lao¹ ping³, to cook a pie. 油炸 iu²-cha², fried in the oil.

TRANSLATION

Turn the pie, cook the pie — the pie with stuffing fried in oil — turn it round and let us see.

LII

高 高 山 上 一 落 磚 兒
磚 兒 上 坐 着 個 老 太 太 兒
三 根 頭 髮 馬 尾 纂 兒
一 心 要 戴 個 涼 涼 簪 兒

NOTES

一落磚兒 i¹ luo¹ chuan¹'r, a pile of bricks 馬尾纂兒 ma³ i³ tsuan³ 'r, sort of sham chignon made of the hair of a horse tail. — 心 i¹ hsin¹, she has no other thought but, compare latin *"toto corde"*. 涼涼簪兒 summer hair-pins; during the summer ladies are supposed to lay aside silver-pins and to wear jade pins and also jade bracelets and rings. People who cannot afford to buy jade pins, get for a trifling sum pins made of glass, imitating the jade. These last are called liang² liang² tsan¹'r.

TRANSLATION.

On a very high mountain there is a pile of bricks. — On the bricks there is sitting an old lady — with three hairs and a false horse-tail chignon — and she only thinks that she wants to wear summer pins on her hair.

LIII

鞋窪兒
厚底兒幫兒
我到娘家走一百
哥哥說炕上坐熱
嫂子說炕不板凳
哥哥說搬不動
嫂子說搬椅子
哥哥說搬腿子
嫂子說沒給妹妹點兒錢
哥哥說還半年
嫂子說還給妹妹點兒米
哥哥說還不起
嫂子說不吃你們的飯
我也不喝你們的酒
我也不親娘我就走
驏賺親娘我就走

出 門 兒 遇 見 個 大 黃 狗
撕 了 我 的 裙 兒
咬 了 我 的 手
忍 心 的 哥 哥 出 來 打 打 狗

NOTES

Chinese wives are allowed from time to time to visit their old family, and to stay there for some days. Here this song depicts the grief of a wife who goes to visit her mother, arrived there she meets with her brother who treats her well and with her sister-in-law who hates her. The words are simple and touching. 厚底兒鞋 hou⁴ ti³ 'r hsie², shoes with a thick heel. 幫兒窄 pang¹ eur chai³, the heel-band is narrow, and therefore it is painful to walk. Pang¹eur is "the leather heel-band of a shoe, for strengthening the back of a shoe" (Giles). 娘家 niang² chia¹, a wife's family. 走 一 百 tsou³ i⁴ pai³ I walk a hundred, it is understood 里 地 li³ ti⁴, chinese miles. The k'ang⁴, chinese brick bed is warmed during winter by fuel. 板凳 pan³ teng⁴, a wooden stool. 還半年 huan² pan⁴ nien², it may be understood so " to give her a little money we shall borrow it and then we shall not be able to repay it back until after a good half-year". 還不起 huan² pu⁴ ch'i³, in the same meaning, we shall not be able to give it back to the person who lends the rice to us. The expression pu⁴ ch'i³ following the verb, that verb acquires a negative potential meaning, as not

6

to be able to... or better corresponding to the Chinese, "not to be up to..." 忍 心 jen¹ hsin¹, these words are a reproach to the brother, meaning you who may tolerate in your heart that I suffer so much, meaning that the brother after all his good intentions lets his wife do as she likes.

TRANSLATION

With high-heeled shoes — and narrow heel-bands — I walk a hundred *li* to arrive at my home, — My elder brother says: Sit on the k'ang¹ — my sister-in-law says: the k'ang is not warm — my elder brother says: bring here a wooden stool — my sister-in-law says: it cannot be brought round — my elder brother says: bring here a chair — my sister-in-law says: the chair has no legs — my elder brother says: give your younger sister some money — the sister-in-law says: we would take half a year to pay it back — my elder brother says: give your gounger sister a little rice — the sister-in-law says, we could not give it back to the lender — But I will not eat your rice — and I will not drink your wine — I will only see my mother and then go away — going out of the gate I have met with a big yellow dog — that has torn my apron — and has bitten my hand — My patient elder brother, come out and beat the dog!

LIV

廮搭家　　母哭穀
甚嘎人　　丈別斗
作瞎給　勸你二來母有兒
兒花丫剪會哭哭過丈還米粥
樹頭子了
黎白活起搭也也婿母家小豆
杜開養拿嘎爹娘女丈我碾熬

餓　不　死　你　的　禿　丫　頭

NOTES

These words are sung to small girls by their
parents. The first two verses have nothing to do
with the rest, but, as a girl is the subject of the
song, they fit very well. 杜黎兒 tu⁴ li⁴ 'r, a pear
with small fruit (*Pyrus betulaefolia*). 瞎嘎搭 hsia¹
ka² ta¹, familiar expression, it means to make noise
using a pair of scissors and without good effect,
and it is said of the small girls who begin to learn
how to cut the cloth to make dresses of it. Hsia¹

originally means blind, and then irregularly, badly as a blind man could do. 給 人 家 kei[3] jon[2] chia[1], they give (the parents) her to people, that is to say they get her married. 豆 兒 粥 tou[i] 'r chou, a gruel made of rice and beans. 禿 了 頭 t'u[i] ya[i] t'ou[2] bald-headed servant, title given in the family to small girls, who are generally called by their parents ya[i] huan[2] or 丫 頭 ya[i] t'ou[2]. 餓 不 死 ngo[i] pu[i] ssu[3], negative potential form, she cannot be starved to death.

TRANSLATION

The small pear-tree — has opened its white flowers — to bring to light a small girl — what is the use of it? — she begins first to take the scissors and to cut badly the cloth — then when she has learned to cut the cloth, one must give her up to other people — the father also weeps — the mother also weeps — the bridegroom comes over to console his mother-in-law — and says: mother-in-law, mother-in-law, do not weep — I have got at home three pecks of grain — we will grind the oats — and boil a rice congee with beans — so that your bald-headed daughter shall not be starved to death.

LV

紅 葫 蘆
軋 腰 兒
我 是 爺 爺 的 肉 姣 兒

我是哥哥的親妹子
我是嫂子的氣包兒
爺爺大箱　賠甚麼姑娘
爺爺大櫃　賠甚麼姑娘
奶奶針線　奶奶筐籮兒　賠甚麼姑娘
哥哥花布　哥哥手巾　賠甚麼姑娘
嫂嫂破罈子　嫂嫂爛碓子
打發那了頭嫁漢子

NOTES

The words are supposed to be said by a small girl. 紅葫蘆 hung^2 hu^2 lu^2, red pumpkin; the boys who have not enough money to buy playthings, content themselves with pumpkins which they go whirling about. 軋腰兒 ya^1 yao^1 'r, " with crushed sides" is the name of a sort of pumpkin shaped in the form of two balls placed one on the other. Cutting this pumpkin in the middle one has two cups. As to the relation between these words to what follows, I suppose the girl speaks of herself as of a precious little thing, because that kind of pumpkin is sometimes appreciated by the Chinese who buy the smallest for two or three taels, and wear them on the body as an ornament. 肉姣兒

jou⁴ chiao¹ 'r, lit. "my flesh dear", an endearing term for a little girl, meaning to say: you are my own flesh and blood. 氣包兒 ch'i⁴ pao¹ 'r, curious express'on said of a person who has the privilege of irritating somebody constantly. The literal translation would be "the wrath-bundle". The small girl speaks so because it is generally admitted and practiced in chinese families that the elder brother's wife carries on continual warfare with her sisters-in-law. Afterwards the girl pretends to want to know what their relations will give her on her wedding day. To give cadeaux to a bride to form her dowry is called 賠 p'ei², or more completely 賠 送 p'ei² sung⁴. 奶奶 nai³ nai,³ one's father's mother. The bannermen call nai³ nai³ a mother. 針線笸籮 chen¹ hsien⁴ p'uo³ luo², a basket where needles, pin, thread, scissors are kept and everything else required for ladies' work. 姑娘 ku¹-niang², is here used instead of the personal pronoun thou or you. 罈子 t'an¹ tzŭ, a big bottle to contain salt vegetables, water and also coal. 罐子 kuan⁴-tzŭ, other sort of vessel made of porcelain or of earthenware. 嫁漢 子 chia⁴ han⁴ tzŭ to marry a husband, a man. Here it would perhaps be better to translate "a fellow" as the woman's words are not inspired with friendly feelings altogether.

TRANSLATION

The red pumpkin — has crushed sides — I am my grandfather's "own dear flesh and blood" —

I am my brother's "carnal sister" — and I am my
sister-in-law's "bundle of wrath" — grandfather,
grandfather, what will you give me at my marriage?
— "I will give you a big chest and a big wardrobe"
— "Grandmother, grandmother, what will you give
me?" — "I will give you a work basket" — "Elder
brother, elder brother, what will you give me?" —
"I will give you a fancy cloth towel" — Sister-in-
law, sister-in-law, what will you give me?" — "A
broken jar — and a smashed bottle — and send you,
that girl, away to marry a fellow".

LVI

黑　兒　葉　樹
煤　子　哟　呀　呀
逵　李　像　的　長　兒　黑　小
兒　眼　着　瞪　兒　牙　着　呇
兒　杆　鞭　黑　個　着　揹　裏　手
兒　牛　黑　着　騎
兒　餠　麵　黑　個　着　喫
兒　頂　山　在　上　上　一

NOTES

These words are sung to children of a brown
complexion. The second verse is simply a refrain
with no meaning. 小黑兒 hsiao³ hei¹ 'r, nickname

given to a brown child.   The word hei¹ contains all
the shades of colour from black to brown. 李逵
Li³ k'uei², a celebrated brigand in the Sung dynasty,
who was of a brown complexion.   He is spoken of
in the Novel 水滸 shuei³ hu³.   His nickname was 黑
旋風 hei¹hsüan² feng¹, the black whirlwind.   呲着牙
tzŭ¹ cho¹ ya², showing the teeth.

TRANSLATION

·The tree-leaves are dark — yaya yüetzu mei —
the small brown boy is very like Li-k'uei — showing
his teeth and staring — he grasps in his hand a
black whip-stick — he rides on a black ox — eats a
cake made of black flour — and going up he gets as
far as the mountain summit.

———————

LVII

荊 條 棍 兒
用 處 兒 多
編 了 柳 斗 兒
編 笆 籮
笆 籮 剆 比 柳 斗 兒 大
管 着 柳 斗 兒 叫 哥 哥

NOTES

荊 ching¹ is instead of 荊蒿花 ching¹ hao¹ hua¹,
the *Vitex incisa*, with stems of which baskets are

woven. 柳斗 liou³ tou³, a measure made of willow branches; sometimes it is made of *Vitex* stems, but it is even then called a "willow-peck". 管着 kuan³-cho¹, with regard to, giving a denomination. 荊條棍兒 ching¹ t'iaɔ² kun⁴ 'r stems of *Vitex*.

TRANSLATION

The stems of the *Vitex incisa* — are fit for many uses — one may make of it a "willow-peck" — and one may make of it a basket — the basket is indeed larger than the willow-peck — and calls the willow peck "elder brother".

LVIII

鐵簍豆
大把兒抓
娶了個媳婦兒就不要媽
要媽就要叉
要叉就分家

NOTES

The first two verses with which the song begins are called 頭子 t'ou² tzɪ "head". They do not seem to have here any relation with the meaning of the following words. The song speaks about some cases in which new-married men forget the duty of obedience to their own mother, and want to set up a family by themselves. The words are ironical and there is in them a sense of reproach and grief. 鐵 t'ie³, iron, here "as hard as iron". 蠶豆 ts'an² tou¹, broad beans, which are sold to children on the streets for the modest sum of a ta for a handful. 大把兒 ta⁴ pa³ 'r, a big handful. 耍叉 shua³ ch'a¹, to fight with a pronged stick, metaph. for "to quarrel". 分家 fen¹ chia¹, to set up an autonomous family, to separate from the old stock.

TRANSLATION.

Broad beans as hard as iron — to be had in big handfuls — after having married a wife, then he does not want his mother — if he wanted his mother then they would quarrel — and if they quarrelled, then he ought to separate from the old house.

LIX

娶媳婦兒的
門口兒過
宮燈戳燈十二個
旗鑼傘扇跕兩傍
八個鼓手奏細樂
轎子抬着姑娘走
抬到婆家的大門
進門兒入洞房

去 會 小 新 郞
娶 了 三 年 並 二 載
丫 頭 小 子 沒 處 兒 擺

NOTES,

娶媳婦兒的 ch'ü³ hsi² fu⁴ 'r ti, the persons who go to fetch the bride and take her to the bridegroom's house. A marriage procession. 宮燈 kung¹ teng¹, "palace lanterns" a sort of lanterns taken in hand by people in the marriage cortège. They are made with silk, or glass doors, and have no lighted candles in them. 戳燈 ch'uo¹ teng¹, another kind of lanterns fixed on a long stick, which may be stuck in the ground. 鼓手 ku³ shou³, literally "drum-hands" general name for all musicians who accompany the bride-chair. Some beat drums, other play on a sort of trumpet called 鎖吶 suo³ na¹. These men are also called 吹鼓手的 ch'ui¹ ku³ shou³ ti. 奏樂 tsou⁴ yüe⁴, to play solemn music. 細樂 hsi⁴ yüe⁴, a concert, a supposed harmony produced by different instruments. 婆家 p'uo² chia¹, mother-in-law, mother-in-law's family, in the husband's family. 小新郞 hsiao³ hsin¹ lang², the young bridegroom. 二載 two years. 三年並二載 san¹ nien² ping⁴ eur⁴ tsai³, a curious expression to mean 5 years.

TRANSLATION

The bridal procession — passes by the gate —

there are twelve "palace lanterns" and "fixed lanterns"—banners, gongs, umbrellas, fans are on each side — eight musicians produce music — the chair which contains the girl passes on — and brings her as far as her mother-in-law's family house-gate — she enters the door and goes into the bridal room — she goes to stay with her young bridegroom — after having married her these five years there are so many babies and girls that there is no more room in the house for them.

LX

長兒窩補要吃黎
巴婦吃錢要閒兒驢集黎皮
尾媳要閒兒驢集黎皮
雀了媽有婦上趕了
喜娶媽沒媳備去買打
不兒補要吃
要薄籬黎
娘脆
媳婦兒媳婦兒你吃黎

NOTES

This song is inspired by the same feeling as song N°. 58. 窩兒薄脆 uo¹ 'r pao² ts'uei⁴, sort of very hard and cheap cake. 笊籬 chao¹ li², a big spoon made of willow stems and used to take food out of the pan. The current phrase "we have no idle money to mend the willow spoon" means that a person has no intention of spending money for useless things, as would be to mend a willow spoon. 打 皮 ta³ p'i², to peel a fruit.

TRANSLATION

The magpie has a long tail — after he has taken a wife he no more wants his mother — when his mother wants to eat some cheap cake — then (he says) "there is no idle money to mend willow spoons" — when his wife wants to eat pears — then he gets ready his ass — and goes to the market — when he has bought the pears — he peels them — and asks wife, wife, will you eat pears?

LXI

小 秃 兒
長 檁 兒
你 媽 養 活 一 對 雙 棒 兒
多 大 了
會 走 咧
你 媽 肚 子 裏 又 有 咧

NOTES

These words are addressed by one boy to another

in a joking way. 小禿兒 hsiao³ t'u¹ 'r, the small baldhead, the boy, used here instead of the personal pronoun "you". 長懞兒 chang³ yang⁴ 'r, he is grown up, lit. "his figure has grown". 養活 yang³ huo², to bear of women; it means also to nourish, to give food. 雙棒兒 shuang¹ pang⁴ 'r, twins, in literary language they are called 雙生 shuang¹ sheng¹.

TRANSLATION

You small bald-heads — are grown up — your mother has born a couple of twins — how old are they? — "they can walk" — "your mother is again in the family way".

LXII

花 紅 柳 緑 線 兒
又 買 針 兒
又 買 線 兒
又 買 王 媽 媽 褲 腿 帶 兒

NOTES

These words are for young girls who want to begin to work early with needle and thread. 花紅 hua¹ hung², as red as red flowers are. 柳緑 liou³ lü⁴, as green as willow-trees are 褲腿帶兒 k'u⁴ t'uei³ tai⁴ 'r, cloth bands used by women to bind the trowsers to their ankles.

TRANSLATION

I want red thread as red as red flowers and
green thread as green as green willows — and I
want to buy needles — and to buy more thread —
and to buy ankle-bands (for) mother Wang.

LXIII

糊 糊
糊 狗 肉 嘔
大 鍋 裏 香
二 鍋 裏 臭
請 王 媽 媽 來 吃 狗 肉 嘔

NOTES

Dog meat is a much appreciated dish in China.
The character 糊 hu², is used here in want of
another, and is pronounced hu¹, in the first tone.   It
means a special chinese way of preparing meat, by
smearing it with sauce and then having it roasted
in a pan.   There is in the western city a restaurant
called 狗 肉 居 kou³ jou¹ chü¹, where roasted dog
meat is provided for " amateurs ".   嘔 ou¹, phonetic
character with no meaning here.

TRANSLATION

Roast, roast — roast dog meat, oh ! — the first

pan smells — and the second pan stinks — I beg
mother Wang to come and eat dog meat, oh !

LXIV

秃 秃 鑔
光 光 鍦
廟 裏 的 和 尚 無 頭 髮
你 摺 磚 兒
我 摺 瓦 兒
單 打 和 尚 的 秃 光 把 兒

NOTES

Chinese boys do not show much reverence
towards the priests, for whom they always have a
ready collection of songs, epigrams and epithets.
One of the general names with which Buddhist
priests are gratified is 秃 驢 t'u¹ lu², a bald ass.
鑔 ch'a¹, small cymbals used as toys; there is no
character for the word and I used, in fault of better,
this character; its original tone however is the first.
As these cymbals are very bright and shining, the
pates of bonzes are likened to them. 秃 光 把 兒
t'u¹ kuang¹ pan³ 'r, a bald and shining pate.

TRANSLATION

Bald bald cymbals — shining, shining cymbals

the bonzes in the temple have no hair — you fling
bricks and I fling tiles — only to strike the bonzes'
bald pates.

LXV

煤 模 兒 　　　　杜 棃 子
炒 豆 兒 　　　　咕 咕 眱 兒

NOTES

Coal dust is mixed up with sand and water and
then put into small wood square boxes, out of which
the coal comes in the form of a small brick.　This
sort of coal is called 煤 黹 兒 mei² chien³ 'r.　When
pekinese boys are so lucky as to get hold of one of
those wood-boxes called 煤 模 兒 mei² mu² 'r, they
put inside of it all their small property, as toys, or
food. 咕 咕 眱 兒, ku¹ ku¹ tiu¹ 'r, seeds of dates.

TRANSLATION

(In) the coal-mould — (there are) roast beans
— small pears — and date seeds.

LXVI

丫 頭 丫
會 看 家

米蘇細蜜糕燒

老芝蘇燉兒火

偷換芝油棗熱撐 的 了 頭 叫 姥 姥

NOTES

油燉蜜 iuᵃ chaᵃ miᵗ, sort of sweet cake made of flower, sugar and honey, and then fried in oil. 棗兒糕 tsao³ 'r kao, pudding of date jam. 火燒 huo³ shaoᵗ, "roasted on the fire" name of a cake. 撐的 ch'engᵗ ti, with a full stomach from having eaten too much.

TRANSLATION

The small girl — knows how to watch the house — she steals old rice — and barters it for sesamum seeds — the sesamum seeds are small — (and then) a sweet cake — a date-pudding — and a roasted cake — the small girl feels so overeaten that she calls for her grandmother.

LXVII

塔瓏玲

瓏玲塔

玲瓏寶塔十三層，
塔前有座玲瓏廟，
廟內有老僧，
老僧當方丈，
方丈名頭頭僧，
頭頭僧點葫蘆，
葫蘆會，會會把弇，
弇把青頭愣僧點葫蘆，
青頭愣僧把磬、管、鐃、鈸，說念法經。

NOTES

玲瓏 ling² lung², elegant, pleasant, smart. 老僧 lao³ seng¹, an old buddhist priest. 方丈 fang¹ chang⁴, the abbot in a buddhist monastery. 徒弟 t'u² ti⁴, pupils who are supposed to learn the law and read the sacred books to become priests afterwards. 青頭愣 ch'ing¹ t'ou² leng⁴, expression impossible to translate; it is applied by Chinese in a despising sense to different objects, as for instance to an unripe fruit, or to a scorpion. 磬 ch'ing⁴ a musical stone used as a bell. 笙 sheng¹, a sort of pipe. 捧 笙 p'eng³ sheng¹, to hold the sheng near the mouth by the two hands, that is to say, to play the sheng. 管 kuan³, a flute. 撞 鐘 chuang⁴ chung¹, to strike the bell; chinese bells are not provided with a clapper, but are struck from outside by means of a wood truncheon hanging by cords at a small distance from the bell. 說 法 shuo¹ fa⁴, to speak about the law, to recite a pious sermon.

TRANSLATION

How elegant is the pagoda! — how the pagoda is elegant! — the elegant pagoda has thirteen stores — before the pagoda there is a temple — in the temple there is an old bonze — the old bonze acts as abbot — and has by himself six pupils — one is called — Ch'ing¹ t'ou² leng⁴. — one is called Leng⁴ t'ou² ch'ing¹ — one is Seng¹ seng¹ tien³ — one is Tien³ tien³ seng¹ — one is P'en¹-hu²-lu²-pa⁴ — one is Pa⁴-hu²-lu²-pən¹ — Ch'ing² t'ou² leng⁴ can strike the musical stone — Leng⁴ t'ou² ch'ing¹ can play the pipe — Seng¹-seng¹-tien³ can play the flute — Tien³ tien³ seng¹ can strike the bell — Pen¹-hu²-lu²-pa⁴ can recite a sermon — and Pa⁴-hu²-lu²pen¹ can read the sacred books.

LXVIII

雄 雞 翎
抱 馬 城

馬 城 開
了 頭 小 子 送 馬 來

NOTES

The military officers in the preceding dynasties used to wear on their hats feathers of the ringed pheasant *(Phasianus torquatus)* called 雉 雞 翎 chib¹ chi¹ ling². The boys of the present day like to ape these old fashions and stick on their hats some cock feathers, which they suppose to be those of the pheasant. Then some of them have a pasteboard horse's head, and horse's rump; the first they tie to the stomach, the other to the back, and their infantile imagination is quite satisfied, as they gallop here and there singing these verses the meaning of which is very doubtful. The pasteboard horse has inside a frame of bamboo sticks and is called 竹 馬 chu² ma³.

TRANSLATION

With ringed pheasant feathers — I gallop to the horse city — the city opens the gate — and girls and boys come out leading a horse for me.

LXIX

藍 靛 廠
四 角 兒 方

宮門口緊對着六郎莊
羅鍋兒橋怎麼那麼高
香山跑馬好熱鬧
金山銀山萬壽山
皇上求雨黑龍潭

NOTES

This song has no other aim then that of collecting names of places in Peking and near Peking. 藍靛廠 lan² tien¹ ch'ang³ the indigo factory, name of a place near Ta-chung-ssu; the ground is now occupied by military quarters for bannermen. 宮門口 kung¹ men² k'ou³, is the name of a street near the P'ing-tse-men. 六郎莊 liu⁴ lang² chuang¹ "the Liou⁴ lang²'s" farm. A place to the South of Yüan²-ming²-yüan². As a matter of fact the Kung¹ men² k'ou³ street and this farm cannot face one another because the street is inside of the city and the farm is in the Hai³-tien⁴. 羅鍋橋 luo² kuo¹ ch'iao², the hunchbacked bridge in Yüan²-ming²-yüan² (see song N° 34). 香山 hsiang¹ shan¹ "perfumed mountains" hills near Peking. 跑馬 p'ao³ ma³, the place in which military men train themselves to shoot arrows whilst galloping on horseback. 金山 chin¹ shan¹, gold mountain, name of another hill in the neighbourhood of Peking. 萬壽山 uan⁴ shou⁴ shan¹, a favourite imperial villa on a hill near Peking. It was once permissible to visit the grounds but now foreigners are no longer admitted. 求雨 ch'iu² yü³ to pray for rain, as the

Emperor in time of drought does himself or by deputy, according to the gravity of the situation. 黑龍潭 hei¹ lung² t'an¹, a temple near Peking, so called because in its grounds there is a pool where a black dragon is supposed to live. The Temple is a Government one and in time of drought imperial kins are sent there to pray for rain. In this small song there is no syntaxis; the names are huddled together without distinction or explanation. The last phrase in order to express correctly the sense, ought to say in the simplest form 皇上爲求雨遣官 到黑龍潭 huang² shang⁴ wei⁴ ch'iu² yü³ ch'ien³ kuan¹ tao⁴ hei¹ lung²t'an¹. The chinese original phrase could however be translated " and the temple of Hei-lung-t'an where the Emperor (goes to pray for rain or) sends people to pray for rain". As a matter of fact from Ch'ien² lung² till now no Emporor has gone there in person to pray for rain. He prays now for it in the 大高殿 ta⁴ kao¹ tien⁴, the very high hall, in the interior of the Palace.

LXX

風 來 咯
雨 來 咯
老 和 尙 背 了 鼓 來 咯

NOTES

When a storm is coming on with wind, rain,

and thunders Pekinese boys say these words. The thunder is supposed to be produced by the striking of a big drum like those which the wandering priests take round with them.

TRANSLATION

The wind has come — the rain has come — the old priest with the drum on his back has come.

LXXI

高 高 山 上 一 顆 蒿

兩 個 禿 子 去 耍 刀

兩 把 刀 尖 兒 落 在 葫 蘆 兒 上

一 個 葫 蘆 兩 扇 瓢

NOTES

一顆蒿 i¹ k'o¹ hao¹, a stem of *artemisia*. This 蒿 is for 香蒿 hsiang¹ hao¹. 禿子 t'u¹-tzŭ, small boys, as explained before. 耍刀 shua³ tao¹, to fence, to play with swords. 兩扇瓢, two gourd ladles-a gourd cut in the middle forms two ladles, used by poor people to put the rice in. The vulgar numeral is not 扇 but 個 ko⁴.

TRANSLATION

On a very high mountain there is a stem of Artemisia — two boys fence with swords — the two

sword points fell on a calabash — and from a
calabash were made two ladles.

LXXII

香爐兒
瓦燈臺
爺爺兒娶了個奶奶兒來
不梳頭
不作活
嘴饞手懶竟愛喝
爺爺兒沒法兒治
氣的竟哆嗦
說我打你這個拙老婆

NOTES

The first two verses are the ordinary t'ou²-tzu
without any reference to what follows. 香爐兒
hsiang¹ lu² 'r, a metal or clay vessel to burn incense
before the Gods; it means literally perfume-stove.
瓦燈臺 ua³ teng¹ t'ai², a sort of earthenware oil-
lamp used in very poor houses. 氣的 ch'i¹-ti, he is
so irritated. 哆嗦 tuo¹ suo¹, to tremble, to shake
with anger.

TRANSLATION

An incense-stove and an earthenware lamp —

the gentleman has married a lady — who does not comb her hair — does not work — is gluttonous and lazy and likes nothing but drinking — the husband has no way of correcting her — and is so angry that he trembles — and says : I will beat you stupid old woman !

LXXIII

小 妞 兒　　錐 幫 子 兒
坐 椅 子 兒　　衲 底 子 兒

NOTES

Girls in poor families make their own shoes. 錐 幫 子 chui[1] pang[1] tzŭ, to bore with an awl holes into the cloth for binding it to the sole. 衲 底 子 na[4] ti[3]-tzŭ, to beat the sole to harden it. The sole is made of felt.

TRANSLATION

The little girl — is sitting on the chair — bores the sides of the shoe — and beats the sole of the shoe.

LXXIV

爺 爺 抱 孫 于
坐 在 波 棱 蓋 兒

羊肉包子蘸醋蒜兒
吃完了撒嬌兒
過來打你爺爺三嘴巴兒

NOTES

蘸 chan[1], to dip in, said of a brush in the ink, or of meat in the sauce. 醋蒜兒 ts'u[4] suan[1] 'r, sort of sauce made of vinegar and bits of garlic. 撒嬌兒 sa[1] chiao[1] 'r, to gambol, to tease, said of spoilt children. 嘴巴 tsuei[3] pa[1], a blow in the face.

TRANSLATION

The grandfather embraces his grandson — who sits on his knees — (the grandfather says) here are meat-balls to dip in vinegar sauce — when you have finished eating you will be saucy — and will come over to hit your grandfather three blows in the face.

LXXV

小脚兒娘
愛吃糖
沒錢兒買
搬着小脚兒哭一場

NOTES

搬脚 pan¹ chiao³, to sit down with crossed legs holding the feet in the hands. Children often sit so when disappointed and weeping.

TRANSLATION.

The little lady with the small feet — likes to eat sugar — but has no money to buy it — and sits crosslegged and weeps for a good while.

LXXVI

高高山上一座樓
兩個姑娘去梳頭
大姐梳的盤龍髻
二姐梳的賽花樓
三姐梳的沒梳了
一個獅子滾繡毯
大姐坐的是金板凳
二姐坐的是銀板凳
剩下三姐沒的坐
一大坐在一盤磨
大姐抱着個金娃子
二姐抱着個銀娃子

三 姐 沒 得 抱
一 抱 抱 着 個 樹 磕 杈

NOTES

盤 龍 髻 p'an² lung² chi¹, sort of women's head dress; literally coiled dragon chignon. 賽 花 樓 sai¹ hua¹ lou², another sort of head dress very high and adorned with flowers; it means literally "tower which emulate the flowers". 獅 子 滾 繡 毯 shih¹ tzǐ kun³ hsiou¹ ch'iu², "a lion who rolls an embroidered ball" sort of amusement in the fairs. Two men dress themselves as lions and then fight, in the same time pushing with the feet a large embroidered ball. Here the phrase is used in the meaning of "confused, not well done, ruffled". — 盤 磨 i¹ p'an² muo⁴, a mill-stone.

TRANSLATION

On a very high mountain there is a high tower — two girls go there to comb their hair — the eldest sister combs her hair into a "coiled dragon chignon" — The second sister combs her hair into a "rivalling flowers tower chignon" — the third sister has no other way of combing her hair — and combs it in a ruffled way — the first sister sits on a golden stool — the second sister sits on a silver stool — there remains the third sister who has no room to sit — and sits on a stone-mill — the first sister folds in her arms a golden baby — the second sister folds in her arms a silver baby — the third sister has nothing to fold in the arms — and folds a forked branch.

LXXVII

駱駝駱駝噻噻
王八是你哥哥
駱駝駱駝拜拜
王八是你太太
駱駝駱駝抽鼻兒
王八是你小姨兒

NOTES

Pekinese boys address these words to camels, which are well tempered enough not to take any notice of them. 噻噻 so¹ so¹, signal given to the camels to make them kneel down, to receive the load on their back. The word is probably derived from the word *sok* used by Mongol camel drivers. The same word is however used to call a dog to come. 拜拜 pai⁴ pai⁴, to salute as women do; here the words refer to the awkward movement of the camels when kneeling down. 抽鼻兒 ch'ou¹ pi² 'r, to sniff, as camels use to do. 小姨兒 hsiao³ i² 'r, a man's wife's younger sister.

TRANSLATION

Camel, camel, kneel down — a turtle is your older brother — camel, camel, make a salute — a turtle is your wife — camel, camel, sniff — a turtle is your sister-in-law.

LXXVIII

七 媽 你
八 媽 我
你 媽 小 脚 兒 開 黃 花
左 一 盤 兒
右 一 盤 兒
你 媽 肚 子 裏 有 小 孩 兒
多 大 了
曾 走 了
你 媽 肚 子 裏 又 有 了

NOTES

Two things are to be observed in the first two verses. Apparently there is nothing wrong in them but it is quite the contrary. Ladies generally avoid pronouncing in succession the numbers seven ch'i[1] and eight pa[1], because, these two syllabes put together, give a sound very similar to that of an

equivocal word largely spoken by Chinamen. Now
in this case the two syllabes are separated but no
Chinese will fail to understand the meaning of it, so
much more that translating the numerals simply as
they are, would convey no meaning in the two first
verses. Again-the word 八 that is to say the
number eight, has been chosen by Chinese to mean
what in higher style would be called 玉 門 yü⁴ men².
Therefore the meaning of the second verse cannot
be an edifying one. 開黃花, k'ai¹ huang² hua¹, "to
open yellow flowers" it seems that in Pekinese
slang a "yellow flower foot" means a small foot.
— 盤 兒 i¹ p'an² 'r, a tour, a walk.

TRANSLATION

Your mother "seven" — your mother "eight"—
your mother has small feet — a tour to the left —
and a tour to the right — your mother is in a family
way — "how old is the baby"? — "he can walk"
— your mother is again in a family way.

LXXIX

桃 樹 葉 兒 尖
荷 花 葉 兒 圓
梔 子 開 花 兒 喚 牡 丹
仙 人 掌 手 拿 三 棱 兒 草
淑 氣 花 開 挨 了 一 頓 弼 王 鞭

NOTES

仙人掌 hsien[1] jen[2] chang, a cactus, (*Opuntia Dillenii*). 三棱草 san[1] leng[2] ts'ao[3], lit. "grass with three edges" a three-cornered sedge *(Cyperus)*. 淑氣花 shu[2] ch'i[4] hua[1], called in vulgar language 蜀角 shou[2] chiao[4] (the original pronunciation and tones ought to be shu[3] chiao[3]), the hollyhock (lat. *Althœa rosea*). 覇王鞭 pa[4] uang[2] pien[1], tyrant's whip, a sort of cactus, called so because of its resemblance to an iron whip property of a king of the Ch'u 楚 kingdom, renowned for his bodily strength, named 項羽 Hsiang[4] yü[3]. In the last verse the phrase has a double meaning as 挨 — 頓鞭 ai[2] i[4] tun[4] pien[1], means to receive a number of whip blows.

TRANSLATION

The peach tree leaves are pointed — the lotus leaves are round — the gardenia opens its flowers and calls the peony tree flower — the cactus (the wise man's palm) holds in its hands the three cornered sedge — the hollyhock flower opens and receives a good many blows from the "tyrant's whip".

LXXX

小 小 子 兒
拿 倒 鍾 兒

兒
門子兒
扇椅子兒
兩漆椅子
子兒搭子兒
屋子脚着壼子兒
怯椑子着壼子兒菜嫩蝦鴨娘席娘
景
名菜兒
有韭菜兒
韭仁子兒
是擺素飽吃
個道席了
人兒
兒
開仙登滿窠檬根大猪上下聲南大蕉蚊子兒
燴燒大葷大台戲扇子兒
開八足水洗四嫩八燒天撤叫上聽芭打

NOTES

拿倒 na² tao⁴, to hold a thing just in the opposite way form that in which it ought to be held, for instance taking a sword by the point. 錘 ch'ui², a toy for boys which imitates an ancient weapon to be seen now only on the theatres, it is formed of a large ball of iron to which is attached a handle, and can be compared to our mace used in the middle ages. 怯屋子 ch'ie⁴ wu¹ tzǔ, a common, plain room, as of labourers in the fields. 八仙棹子 pa¹ hsien¹ chuo¹ tzǔ, a table for eight persons. 漆椅子 ch'i¹ i³ tzǔ, lacquered chairs. 脚搭子 chiao³ ta¹ tzŭ, a small four-legged stool to lay the feet on. 窜子 ts'uan¹ tzŭ, very vulgar name for a kettle. 名景 ming² ching³, fame, renown. 嫩根兒 nen¹ ken¹'r, with delicate stems. 韭菜 chiou³ ts'ai⁴, leeks. 八大 pa¹ ta¹ instead of 八大碗 pa¹ ta¹ wan³, the eight entries in a good chinese dinner. The verse is very laconic. 燴蝦仁兒 huei⁴ hsia¹ jen²'r, shrimp pulp with sauce. 天上大娘 t'ien¹ shang¹ ta⁴ niang², a fairy in heaven, but here very probably a term of flattery for a nun. 道人兒 tao⁴ jen²'r, said also in relation to above, a person who has reached the perfection of reason, a holy person. 葷席 hun¹ hsi², a dinner comprising meat and food, which persons in monastic life should abstain from eating. 南台 nan² t'ai², the theatre placed on the Southern side. 芭蕉 pa¹ chiao¹, palm tree、打蚊子 ta³ uen²-tzŭ, to drive away the sandflies.

TRANSLATION

The small boy — holding the mace by the head — opens the two leaves of the door of the plain room — (inside there are) one table for eight people and varnished chairs — he leans his feet on a small footstool — the tea pot is overfilled with water — and washes the kettle — four sorts of food are there spread out — delicate leeks with delicate stems — and eight plates with sauced shrimp pulp — pork with sauce and roasted duck — (the nun) like the great lady in heaven is a holy person — and she has the common food removed and vegetable food prepared — people call out: the great lady has eaten to fullness — and goes to the Southern stage — to see the play — and with a palm-leaf fan — strikes away the mosquitoes.

LXXXI

高 高 山 上 一 顆 蔴
有 個 吉 了 兒 往 上 爬
我 問 吉 了 兒 爬 怎 的
他 說 渴 了 要 吃 蔴

NOTES

吉了兒 chi² liao³'r, the cicada, correctly written 蜘蟟兒. 怎的 tsen³ ti, antiquated form for 怎麼着 tsem³ mo cho, how? why? 吃蔴 ch'ih¹ ma², to eat hemp, a curious way of letting thirst pass away.

TRANSLATION

On a very high mountain there is a stem of hemp — there is a cicada who creeps on it — I ask the cicada, why do you creep on? — and she says: I am thirsty and want to eat hemp.

LXXXII

好 熱 天 兒
掛 竹 簾 兒

歪 脖 兒 樹 底 下
有 個 妞 兒 哄 着 我 頑 兒
穿 着 一 件 大 紅 坎 肩 兒
沒 有 沿 邊 兒
梳 油 頭
別 玉 簪 兒
左 手 拿 着 玉 花 籃 兒
右 手 拿 着 梔 子 茉 莉 串 枝 蓮 兒

NOTES

歪脖兒樹 uai¹ puo²'r shu⁴, "trees with a crooked neck" crooked trees. 大 紅 ta⁴ hung², deep red. 沿邊兒 yen² pien¹'r, coloured border of ladies dresses. 油頭 iu² t'ou² a hairdress combed with odorous oil. 別 pie², there is no particular character for the meaning; it means to wear pins in the hair as women do. 花籃兒 hua¹ lan²'r, a flower basket.

TRANSLATION .

What a hot day — set up the bamboo curtain! — under the crooked trees — there is a small girl who plays and jests with me — she wears a deep red waistcoat — without coloured border — she has combed her hair with oil — and has stuck jade pins into her hair — in the left hand she holds a flower basket — and in the right hand she holds gardenias, jasmine and wild lotus flowers.

LXXXIII

羊 巴 巴 蛋 兒
用 脚 撮
你 是 兄 來 我 是 哥
打 壺 酒 兒 偺 們 倆 人 喝
喝 醉 了
打 老 婆
吹 鼻 兒 打 鼓 再 娶 一 個

NOTES

The beginning of this song is nasty but I could not cut it off the song. 羊巴巴蛋兒 yang² pa³ pa³ tan¹r, goat dung — 打壺酒兒 ta³ hu² chiou³, to go to buy a bottle of wine. 鼻兒 pi²'r, the mouth of a flute, therefore 吹鼻兒 ch'ui¹ pi²'r, means to play the flute or other wind instrument. This phrase alludes to the band of players which accompanies the chair of a bride.

TRANSLATION

Goat's dung — crushed by the foot — you are my second brother and I am your first brother — go and buy a bottle of wine; we will both drink it — when I am drunk — I will beat my wife — and then with flute-players and drummers I will marry another.

LXXXIV

兒
號兒
吹兒哇少吊兒了小懊兒少少兒兒
廟兒嗢春哇年兩罷了的好票少少兒
小道兒嗢青元嗢春兒少泡
個神兒轎兒個張罷兒的好
有個帽兒兒抬轎兒個張元兒罷兒還你心票少少泡
上着罩套兒要抬鬼鬼了溜一千兒抱兒抱懷燒鬼間春都
山住草藍皮草小小來提兒懷懷我火花兒小青青咕
高頭戴穿繫個個南裏廟個我給把兒道聲拿的廊
高裏頭身腿腰四兩解手進求給不點灰神呌快嚇咕

NOTES

罩兒 chao'r, very thin overcoat which the Chinese

wear over their clothes. 草要兒 ts'ao³ yao⁴'r, sort of rope made of dry grass to bind vegetables together, and in this case as a girdle. 温兒哇 weur¹ wa¹, imitates the sound of the trumpet. 吹號 for 吹號筒 ch'ui¹ hao⁴ t'ung³, to blow the trumpet. 青春 ch'ing¹ ch'un, the pure spring, the flower of life, youth. 千張 ch'ien¹ chang¹, a paper ladder burned in ceremonies in order to give the spirits a way to ascend to heaven. 元寶兩吊 yüan² pao³ liang³ tiao⁴, two strings of paper money, resembling the silver yüan-pao, which the Chinese burn for their dead and in other offerings. 懷抱兒 huai² pao⁴'r, something to carry in the bosom, a child. 一把火 i¹ pa⁴ huo³, a bundle of combustible matter for obtaining a fire. 灰兒花兒 hui¹'r hua¹'r, wants to imitate the noise of a conflagration. 發票 fa¹ p'iao⁴, to issue a warrant to arrest a man. 冒泡兒 mao⁴ p'ao⁴'r, to gasp and let air out of the mouth as fish does when just taken out of the water; that is said to show the agonizing fear of the young girl. 咕嘟咕嘟 ku¹ tu¹ ku¹ tu¹, imitates the gurgling round of the air gasping out of the throat.

TRANSLATION

On a very high mountain — there is a small temple — inside is sitting a holy man — who wears on his head a dry grass hat — and on his body an azure cloak — and on his legs skin leggings — and round his waist a grass rope for girdle — four small devils bear the chair — two small devils blow the trumpet — from the South has come a young girl in the bloom of life — who has in her hands a paper ladder and paper money — she enters the temple — to pray for a child — (she says :) give me a child and it shall be all right — if you do not give me a child — I will make a fire — and burn your small temple — the holy man hearing this is very much angry — and calls for the small devils to issue a warrant of arrest — (saying) quickly apprehend this young woman in the bloom of life, — but the young woman in the bloom of life is so scared that she gasps for breath.

LXXXV

有 個 妞 兒 不 害 羞
管 着 賣 花 的 叫 舅 舅
舅 舅 舅 舅 給 我 一 朵 紅 石 榴
懷 裏 揣
袖 裏 袖
利 利 拉 拉 一 大 溜

NOTES

揣 ch'uai, means to feel, to grope, and also to hide in the bosom, as Chinese do because of their not having pockets. 袖 hsiouʻ, a sleeve, and also, to place in the sleeve 利利拉拉 liʻ liʻ laʻ laʻ — without interruption·without end. 一大溜 iʻ taʻ liuʻ, a great row a great number of.

TRANSLATION

There is a small girl who does not feel ashamed — and calls the flower seller her own uncle — uncle, uncle give me a flower of the red pomegranate — I will put it in my bosom — I will put it in my sleeve — and all the ground shall be strown with flowers.

LXXXVI

高
姓燒女毛上　了火怒瓢
本香兒爲毛　掉架冲開
兒把爲香天　毛爺冲刀
禿五香香天　天老見就
小十燒三香　天了一大
個一家燒了　倒爺起
有初人禿到　又到搬老拿
　　　　　　　　燒

NOTES

The Chinese are accustomed to burn incense on the first and fifteenth of a month. 爲長毛 uei¹ chang⁴ mao², to make the hair grow. 掛袍 kua¹ p'ao², " to put on Buddha's body a jacket ". Some people who want to get a favour from the Divinity, to soothe him, buy a silk or satin jacket which they themselves put on his body. 搬倒了 pan¹ tao³ la, he upset the God. 老爺 lao³ ye², Mister, Sir, gentleman, here it is instead of 關老爺 kuan¹ lao³ ye², the God of war. 架 chia⁴, to lean the object on a stand, here in order to burn it completely. 冲冲怒 ch'ung¹ ch'ung¹ nu⁴, in great irritation.

TRANSLATION.

There was a small bald-headed man, whose name was Kao — who went to burn incense on the first and on the fifteenth — people burn incense to get a son or a daughter — but the baldheaded man burns incense to make his hair grow — after three days the hair was growing — and he burns incense — and dresses the God with a new jacket — after three days the hair fell off — and he upset the Kuanti statue and placed him against a stand to burn him — But Kuanti seeing that, was awfully irritated — he took up his great halberd and split the man's calebash (head) into two ladles.

LXXXVII

立 立 立 立 站 兒
上 河 沿 兒
一 個 猪 劈 兩 半 兒
你 一 半 兒
我 一 半 兒
打 酒 就 酒 菜 兒

The first word li̍ is reapeted four times for the sake of the rhythm. 就酒菜兒 chiou⁴ chiou³ ts'ai''r, to accompan ythe food which is generally taken whilst drinking wine; here it alludes to the pig's head.

TRANSLATION

I top here — go on the banks of the river — of a pig's head we will make two portions — you will get a half — and I will get a half — and we will go and buy wine to suit the wine-food.

LXXXVIII

鑼 鍋 兒 橋
萬 壽 山
鎮 海 銅 牛 在 上 邊
賣 豆 腐 腦 兒 的
喝 喝 連 連 在 海 淀

NOTES

This song is not very intelligible; names of places are put together without any apparent reason. 鎮 chen⁴, to protect against bad luck and danger. 鎮物 chen⁴ u⁴, an object which counteracts evil influences. The brass ox which is spoken of here is on the shore of the lake k'un¹ ming² hu² and is there to oppose the danger which chinese believe would arise from the overflowing of the lake. In the lake there is supposed to be a 海眼 hai³ yen³, that is to say a "sea-eye" a hole in the bottom of the lake which communicates with the sea, and out of which all the sea water would rise and overflow the country. The lake 昆明湖 k'un¹ ming² hu² is in the Haitien in the neighbourhood of Peking. 在上邊 tzai⁴ shang⁴ pien¹, on the shore. 豆腐腦 tou⁴ fu³ nao³, sort of bean-curd. 喝喝 ho¹ ho¹, cries of vendors in the street. 連迾 lien² lien², without interruption.

TRANSLATION

The hunchback bridge — Wan-shou-shan — the brass oxen on the shore, which protects the country from the sea water — the vendors of bean curd — go along crying their ware without interruption.

LXXXIX

黑 老 婆 兒
滿 地 滾
嗔 着 他 男 人 不 買 粉
買 了 粉 他 不 搽
嗔 着 他 男 人 不 買 蒜
買 了 蒜 他 不 打
嗔 着 他 男 人 不 買 馬
買 了 馬 他 不 騸
嗔 着 他 男 人 不 買 櫃
買 了 櫃 他 不 盛

嗔 着 他 男 人 不 買 繩
買 了 繩 他 上 弔
嚇 了 他 男 人 一 大 跳

NOTES

滿 地 滾 man³ ti⁴ kun³, rolls all over the ground.
嗔 着 ch'en¹ cho², speaking angrily, scolding. 打 蔴
ta³ ma², to beat the hemp, to take away the bark from
the stems. 盛 here read ch'eng², to fill something
with, to put, to place in. 上 弔 shang⁴ tiao⁴, to hang
oneself.

TRANSLATION

The old brown woman — rolls herself all over
the ground — scolding because her husband does
not buy cosmetic for her — but when he has bought
cosmetic then she does not use it — scolding because her husband does not buy hemp for her — when
he has bought hemp, then she does not thrash it —
scolding because her husband does not buy a horse
— when he has bought a horse, she does not feed
it — scolding because her husband does not buy a
wardrobe — when he has bought the wardrobe, she
does not puts her things there — scolding because
her husband has not bought a cord — when he has
bought a cord, she hangs herself — and frightens
her husband to death.

XC

小小子兒
小咕圇墪兒
胖臂上戴着個金鐲子兒
骹身穿紅兜肚綠褲子兒
腦袋瓜兒梳着個歪毛兒
一笑倆酒窩
一走一哆嗦
拉着姐姐偺們買果子

NOTES

胖咕圇墪兒 p'ang¹ ku¹ lun¹ tun¹'r, fat and round, said of a child. 兜肚 tou¹ tu⁴, a covering for the stomach worn by children. 腦袋瓜兒 nao³ tai⁴ kua¹'r, the head, the skull, a jocular expression. 歪毛兒 uai¹ mao² 'r, a round tuft of hair which small boys wear either on the right or on the left of the head. 酒窩兒 chiu³ uo¹'r, dimples in the cheek.

TRANSLATION

The very little boy — is round and fat — he wears a gold bracelet on his arm — and wears a red stomach protector and green trowsers — on his head he wears a tuft of hair — when he laughs two dimples appear on his cheeks — when he walks all his body trembles — and taking the elder sister by the hand says: elder sister, let us go and buy fruit.

XCI

黄城根兒
一溜門兒
門口兒站着個小妞人兒
有個意思兒
白布汗褟兒藍布褲子兒
耳朵上戴着排環墜兒
頭上梳的是大抓髻兒
搽着胭兒
抹着粉兒
誰是我的小女婿兒

NOTES

皇城 huang² ch'eng², the wall which goes round the imperial city. 城根兒 ch'eng² ken¹'r, near the wall, opposite to it. 妞人兒 niu¹-jen², rather affected for the sake of rhyme instead of the simple 妞兒 niu¹'r. 有個意思兒 iou³ ko⁴ i⁴ ssu¹'r, there is a thought, it is amusing pleasant to look at it and to think of it. 排環墜兒 p'ai² huan² chuei⁴'r, a sort of earrings for women. 搽胭 ch'a¹ yen¹, to rub rose cosmetic on the cheeks or on the palms of the hands. 抹粉 muo³ fen³, to rub white cosmetic powder on the cheeks. 小女婿兒 hsiao³ nu³ hsü⁴, a small son-in-law, said to a girl to mean her bridegroom.

TRANSLATION

Near the wall of the imperial town — there is

a row of doors — near a door there stands a small girl — she is really nice — with a shirt of white cloth and trowsers of blue cloth — she wears round earrings — and has a great chignon on her head — on the face she has rubbed red powder — and white powder — who shall be my little bridegroom ?

XCII

詹 蝙 蝠　　你 是 奶 奶 兒
穿 花 鞋　　我 是 爺

NOTES

The first two verses are the common introduction without definite meaning. 詹蝙蝠 the bat is called in suhua yen¹ pien¹ hu³, but the regular pronunciation ought to be yen² pien¹ fu². As to the fact of wearing embroidered shoes, the chinese explain as follows : sometimes in order to catch a bat, a shoe is thrown in the air, and the bat himself runs into the shoe and so falls to the ground and is taken. Very likely the need of a rhyme has forced in the whole phrase.

TRANSLATION

The bat — wears embroidered shoes — you are a wife — and I am a husband.

XCIII

老 太 太 叫 貓
花 兒 花 兒 花 兒 狐 狸 喲
我 們 的 貓 有 名 兒
鞭 打 繡 球 金 鑲 玉
雪 裏 送 炭 四 個 銀 蹄
有 人 要 偷 了 我 們 的 貓 兒 去
抽 了 你 的 筋 來
剝 了 你 的 皮

NOTES

花兒花兒 hua''r hua'r, is equivalent to the english puss! puss! to call a cat. 花兒狐狸 hua'r hu² li² striped fox-the name of one of the cats belonging to the lady. 鞭打繡球 pien¹ ta³ hsiou⁴ ch'iu², means literally "a whip that beats the embroidered ball". The coats of cats have different curious names to distinguish them. This phrase means a cat which has a black tail and a black spot on the forehead, meaning that with his long black tail (the whip) he strikes the black spot on the forehead (the embroidered ball). 金鑲玉 chin¹ hsiang¹ yü⁴, another name for a cat's coat "jade inlaid with gold" a cat with a white coat with yellow spots. 雪裏送炭 hsüe³ li³ sung⁴ t'an⁴, another name, literally explained "coal sent in the snow" a black coat with four white paws. 銀蹄 in²-t'i², a silver hoof, said of white hoofs and paws.

TRANSLATION

The old lady calls the cat — puss, puss! Fox — our cats have all a name — (there is) "the whip that beats the embroidered ball" and "jade inlaid with gold" — and more "coal brought in the snow" with four white paws — if there is a man who wants to steal away my cat — I will draw out your muscles — and peel away your skin.

XCIV

兒辣嘴下了洗前子臭烟茶媽叫兒氣永遠

椒不爸地流耍往徵說袋我爸太生兒

秦麼爸在怕爸了是過過的爸太要今

小怎我跪還我脫要遞樂我老再從

怕

害蠟

就燃了

媽個摔了

我着兒

兒頂油脚跑還挨兒咎了饒我永遠

香巴

說嘴

牙齦我出不

兒孩去罷我滾

他去

媽家回

NOTES

This song is supposed to be sung by a small boy who innocently relates the strife between father and mother. In China although the family laws are severe and different from ours, yet there exists a sufficient number of henpecked husbands. A number of anecdotes regarding uxorious husbands are currently spread. 秦椒 ch'in² chiao¹, chillies (lat. *Capsicum annuum*); very likely here the house wife is not wrongly likened to the chillies. 爸爸 pa¹ pa¹, common appellation for father, and the same as our papa. 頂着燈 ting³-cho¹-teng¹, bearing a lamp on the head; a henpecked husband is jestingly supposed to kneel down before his wife, who orders him as a punishment to stay a long time in that position, with an oil-lamp on his head. So the husband must endure the pain of being scalded by the oil that drops down from the lamp and runs on his back. This notion is so generally known and jested about that one of the must common tricks to produce general hilarity is to alarm a friend by saying he has got oil-stains on his back. Everybody understands what fictions that alludes to. 油 iu², for oil is intended here the product of the melting of wax. 一袋烟 i¹ tai¹ yen¹, a pipe filled with tobacco. 孩兒他媽 hai²'r t'a¹ ma¹, "the children's mother" title given by the husband to a wife who has born children to him. The wife in her turn calls the husband 孩兒他爸爸 hai²'r t'a¹ pa¹ pa¹, the children's father. Two abridged phrases for that are 他媽 and 他爹.

TRANSLATION

The small chillies — how could they not be
bitter? — when my father catches sight of my mother, he is afraid — he kneels down with a lamp
on his head, — and is also afraid lest the oil should
run down, or the candle should fall — when my
mother wants to wash her feet — my father runs
forward — when he has taken down the socks he
says that it is scented — if he says it is bad smelling
he gets a slap on the face — when he has filled her
pipe — and handed over to her a cup of tea — my
mother is so delighted that she shows her teeth —
my father has once called her : o mother of my
children — old lady, forgive me, now — if you are
going to get angry again, I will roll away — and from
now henceforward I will never come back home.

XCV

蒿 子 燈　　　　今 兒 點
荷 葉 燈　　　　明 兒 個 扔

NOTES

On the fifteenth day of the seventh moon is
celebrated the Feast of the Spirits 中 元 節 chung¹ yüan²
chie². In the evening many lanterns are lighted on
the streets. 蒿 子 燈 hao¹ tză³ təng¹, it is not a lantern
but a whole plant of artemisia on the branches of
which incense sticks are bound and then lighted.

荷葉燈 ho[2] yo[4] teng[1], another lantern formed of a leaf of lotus on which a candle has been fixed.

TRANSLATION

The artemisia lantern — and the lotus-lantern — to day they are lighted — and to-morrow they are thrown away.

XCVI

小三兒他媽
頂历柁
窩摳眼
挺長脖
穿着一件破衫襖
窰窿兒大
補丁多
渾身的鈕子沒有兩個
告訴你媽嫁了我罷
又得吃來又得喝

NOTES

頂 ting[3], to reach with the head. 历柁 fang[2] t'uo[2], the principal beam in the roof. 摳 k'ou[1] means here sunken, deep and 窩摳眼 uo[1] k'ou[1] yen[3], sunken eyes. 挺 t'ing[3], character used to form the superlative in very common language, used instead of 頂 ting[3].

祆 襖 tuo¹ luo², sort of old dress consisting of a long gown with a high collar, worn in winter time.
補 丁 pu³ ting¹, patches. A chinese coat has never more than six buttons.

TRANSLATION

Sar's mother — is as tall as the roof — has sunken eyes — and a very long neck — she wears a broken overcoat — with big holes — and many patches — on her whole person there are not even two buttons — now, tell your mother to marry me! — she will get food and drink.

XCVII

小 耗 子 兒   偷 油 吃
上 燈 台   下 不 來

TRANSLATION

The small mouse — has climbed up the candlestick — to steal oil to eat — and now cannot come down.

XCVIII

兩 枝 蠟
一 股 香
二 十 三 日 祭 竈 王
一 碟 兒 草 料

一　碗　水
潑　在　地　下　上　天　堂　
當　家　的　過　來　把　頭　叩
三　聲　爆　竹　响　叮　噹
竈　王　爺
回　來　罷　回　來　罷
給　你　留　着　關　東　糖

NOTES

This song speaks about the ceremony for the God of the stove on the 23ᵈ day of the twelfth moon. Before the God's picture incense is burning and on the table there is a dish containing water, and one with grass which is supposed to serve for the God's horse. The water then is thrown to the ground and the grass in the air. That means the end of this ceremony. 當家的 tang¹ chia¹ ti, the oldest man in the family who is called to perform the sacrifices and all religious ceremonies. 天堂 t'ien¹ t'ang², the Heavenly hall, the paradise. 爆竹 p'ao⁴ chu², fire crackers. 响叮噹 hsiang³ ting¹ tang¹, the noise is ting-tang; 關東糖 kuan¹-tung¹ t'ang², Manchurian sugar. The Chinese offer sugar to this God, with the aim of letting his teeth stick together and so prevent him from relating to Heaven all the inconvenience and misdeed he had occasion to see in the family during twelve months; with this hope, the Chinese merrily begin their New-year.

TRANSLATION

Two candles — a bundle of incense sticks —
on the 23d day it is sacrificed to the God of the
hearth — there is a dish full of grass — and a dish
full of water — when the water is thrown on the
ground the God ascends to Heaven — the eldest of
the family comes over and knocks his head on the
ground — then three volleys of crackers with a great
noise — God of the hearth — come back! come back!
— we keep for you Manchurian sugar.

XCIX

八 仙 棹 兒
四 角 兒 方
盤 子 碗 兒 擺 在 中 央
燒 豬 燒 鴨 子 東 坡 肉
保 府 帶 來 的 八 寶 香 腸

NOTES

四 角 兒 ssu¹ chiao"r, with four corners. 中 央
chung yang¹, in the middle-the word yang¹ is pronounced vulgarly yang². 東 坡 肉 tung¹ p'uo¹ jou¹, sort of
meat prepared in a special way as directed by a
certain old literary man who was a great authority
also on kitchen matters. His name was 蘇 軾 Su¹-
shih¹ and his surname, hao, was Tung p'uo¹. 保 府
Pao³-fu³ is instead of 保 定 府 Pao³ ting⁴ fu³, the head

prefecture in the Chih-li province. 八寶香腸 pa¹ pao³ hsiang¹ ch'ang² "the odorous sausages with eight treasures" a sort of sausages made of pork stuffed into chicken's intestines. The eight treasures alluded to are the spices, aromas which are in the stuff. These sausages come from Pao-ting-fu.

TRANSLATION

A table for eight persons — with four corners square — plates and cups are placed in the middle of it — roast pork, roast duck, and meat prepared à la Tung-p'uo — and sausages from Pao-ting-fu.

C

喜 兒 喜 兒 吃 豆 腐
小 鷄 兒 過 來 嗛 把 穀
狗 兒 汪 汪 要 看 家
貓 兒 過 來 會 撲 鼠

NOTES

喜兒 hsi²'r stands for 喜雀 hsi³ ch'iao³, the magpie. 嗛 ch'ien¹, to peck. 汪汪 uang⁴ uang⁴, imitates the noise of barking. 撲鼠 p'u¹ shu³, to rush on mice, to catch mice as cats do. These words are repeated by children when they catch sight of magpies.

TRANSLATION

The magpie, the magpie eats beancurd — the chicken comes over and pecks a handful of grain —

the dog barks and wants to look after the house —
the cat comes over and wants to catch the mice.

CI

喜 兒 喜 兒 買 豆 腐
該 我 的 錢
臘 月 二 十 五

NOTES

Chinese accounts and debts are paid at the end
of every quarter and the great bulk of money
accounts ought to be paid, in the 12th month from
the 25th day to the 30th at midnight.

TRANSLATION

The magpie, the magpie buys beancurd — those
who owe me money — (I shall see them) on the 25th
day of the 12th moon.

CII

顧 不 得 一 時 哑 着
你 插 槍
我 撅 鎬
上 南 莊
刨 元 寶

蒲包瞧
大奧寶
個望元寶兩丈高
出包銀鑽兒
刨蒲寶鑽筍子
刨着元鋼大珊瑚
一隔仚金兩珊瑚
要買人怕人逃跑
要買房子怕火燒
要買驢怕倒槽
要開當鋪眼力兒澡
要開錢桿子沒人兒保
東邊兒摸
西邊兒摸
摸了個青頭愣的蝎子
蹩的我鬼哭神嗥

NOTES

The song relates a dream. 顧不得 ku⁴ pu⁴ to², without aperceiving it; insensibly. 鎬 kao³, said also 鐝頭 chüe³ t'ou², a hoe. The first character is not noted in dictionaries. 刨 p'ao², to dig the ground with a hoe. 蒲包 p'u² pao¹, a bundle made of rushes. 金鋼石 chin¹ kang¹ shih², the diamond. 金鋼鑽兒 chin¹ kang¹ tsuan⁴'r, the diamond-pointed awl used by menders of crockery. 倒槽 tao³ ts'ao², said of animals "to die near the manger, in the stable". 眼力兒潮 yen³ li⁴'r ch'ao³, lit. the strenght of the eyes

is damp, that is to say we have not eyes good enough
to distinguish good objects from bad ones - a faculty
which is necessary in such an establishment as a
pawn-shop. The word ch'ao² has also in other cases
the meaning of not up to, insufficient, as in 潮銀子
ch'ao² yin² tzu, bad silver, with too much alloy. 錢棹
子 ch'ien² cho¹-tzu, lit. "money-table" a bank autho-
rized to issue small banknotes and guaranteed by
other banks. 摸 muo¹, to feel with the hands, read
here vulgarly ma:². 鬼哭神嚎 kuei³ k'u¹ shen² hao³,
"the devils weep and the spirits wail" that is "in
a very painful way".

TRANSLATION

Without perceiving it in a moment I fell asleep
— (I dreamed) you had shouldered a gun — and I
shouldered a hoe — and went to the South morass —
to dig out silver ingots — and digging we dug out a
big rush wrapper — through the rush wrapper we
looked in — there were gold ingots and silver ingots
— and two large buckets of diamonds — and two
coral trees two chang high — but if we buy servants
I am afraid they would run away — if we buy houses
I am afraid they would burn — if we buy an ass, I
am afraid he would die near the manger — if we
open a pawn-shop, we have not eyes good enough
for that — if we open a money-shop, there is none
who will guarantee us — but feeling for the East
— and feeling for the West — I felt a big ugly

scorpion — which bit me so painfully that it made me scream.

CIII

小犬姐、

小二姐

你拉胡琴我打鐵

挣了錢兒

腰裏掖

買個蒲包兒贐乾爹

乾爹戴着紅纓帽

乾兒穿着厚底兒鞋

走一步

格登登

扎蝴蝶兒鴨蛋青

NOTES

拉胡琴兒 la¹·hu²·ch'in²·r, to play the tartar fiddle. 打鐵 ta³ t'ie³, to beat the iron, to work the iron. 腰裏掖 yao¹ li³ye¹, to hide, to place something in the waist. — These baskets made of rushes are especially used for containing objects for gifts. 格登登 ko² teng¹ teng¹ imitates the noise of the shoes slapping on the ground. 鴨蛋青 ya¹ tan⁴ ch'ing¹. of the same colour as the eggs of ducks.

TRANSLATION

You the first small young lady — and I the second small young lady — you play on the fiddle — and I will strike the iron — when we will have gained money — we will put it in the waist — we will buy a rush basket and will go to see our adopted father — Our adopted father has a red fringed hat — and our adopted mother has shoes with a thick sole — at every step — the creaking is heard — the butterflies embroidered on the shoes are of duck's egg colour.

CIV

新 姑 娘 十 幾 咯
婆 婆 家 要 娶 了
一 對 兒 龍
一 對 兒 鳳
金 瓜 鉞 斧 朝 天 鐙
小 紅 鞋 兒
蝴 蝶 兒 夢
跳 了 棹 子 上 板 凳

NOTES

The dragon is compared to the bridegroom and the phoenix bird to the bride. In the marriage cortege there are taken round a pair of banners on which the dragon is painted and another pair on which is painted the phoenix. 金瓜 chin¹ kua¹, gilt wood gourd stuck to the end of a pole and taken round. 鉞斧 yüe⁴ fu³, a sort of wooden axe. 朝天鐙 ch'ao² t'ien¹ teng⁴, a stirrup iron turned upside down and stuck on a pole. 小紅鞋兒 hsiao³ hung² hsieᵉ'r, red satin shoes worn by the bride. 蝴蝶兒夢 hu² t'ierᵉ r meng⁴, the Dream of the butterflies, name of a pattern of shoes on which butterflies are embroidered.

TRANSLATION

The bride is ten years and more — the mother-in-law wants to take her home — a pair of dragon flags — and a pair of phoenix flags — and gilt gourds, gilt axes, and reversed stirrups. — (the bride wears) small red shoes — and she jumps on the table and then on the bench.

CV

有邊兒有邊兒眞有邊兒
藍布的大衫兒
靑坎肩兒
時興花兒的褲子賽橙船兒

NOTES

These words describe the toilet of a small girl. 有邊兒 iou³ pien¹'r, slang phrase which means to be very nice, to be first rate. 衫兒 shan¹'r, read here shan³'r, a summer thin bodice. 時 興 shih² hsing¹, the fashion. 賽糧船兒 sai¹ liang² ch'uan²'r, bigger, larger than a ship used to bring the grain tributes.

TRANSLATION

She is first rate, first rate, really first rate! — with a great bodice of azure cloth — and a brown waistcoat — and trowsers with a new pattern, as large as a rice junk.

CVI

出 了 門 兒 好 喪 氣
瞧 了 個 兎 子 倒 慼 氣
剛 要 拿 槍 打
看 了 一 看
是 個 拉 屎 的

NOTES

In Peking, generally acknowledged to be the dirtiest city in the world, it is not an uncommon sight to see people stopping on the public streets to perform the duties of nature. The chinese do not resent it but the boys have composed these few verses which they sing loudly, when the occasion arises

10

of insulting any one caught in the act. 好 hao³ does not mean here good but "how much"! how great! — We have already hinted at the double meaning of the word hare in China. Here the word is not used without a reason; 倒戀氣 tao¹ pie¹ ch'i¹, means to draw in the breath as if preparing for an effort.

TRANSLATION

As soon as I came out of my gate, what an unauspicious sight! — I saw a hare which was drawing in its breath — I was just going to take the gun and shoot — when looking more closely — it was a man who had been taken short!

CVII

咚 咚 咚
坐 轎 兒
一 坐 坐 到 二 廟 兒
二 廟 東
二 廟 西
裏 頭 坐 着 個 肥 公 鷄
哏 哏 哏 兒
上 草 垛

NOTES

咚咚咚 tung¹ tung¹ tung¹, imitates the noise of a drum and 哏兒 imitates the cock's crowing. 草垛 ts'ao³ tuo¹, a heap of straw, of oats.

TRANSLATION

The drums are striking — (she) is sitting in the chair — and has gone as far the second temple — the east of the temple — and the west of the temple — inside there sits a fat cock — which crows — and flies on a heap of straw.

CVIII

一 進 門 兒 黑 咕 窿 咚
先 當 銅 盆 後 當 燈
一 進 門 兒 本 是 一 窩 耗 子 精
說 一 聲 不 好 牆 要 咕 咚

NOTES

The interior of a miserable house is described. 黑 咕 窿 咚 hei¹ ku¹ lung² tung¹ (pronounce with the accent on the last) the first syllabe only gives a clear sense-the other cannot be explained but the general sense is that of complete obscurity, chaos. 耗 子 精 hao⁴ tzǔ ching¹, transformation of mice : fantastical mouse-like elves. 不 好 pu¹ hao³ here alas !

TRANSLATION

Upon entering all was pitch dark — because first the copper basin had been pawned and then the lamp too — going inside (I perceived) I was in a nest of mouse-like elves — and just when I was saying : alas ! here the wall is coming down !

CIX

高高山上一座樓
男人梳着女人頭
狀元及第空歡喜
恩愛夫妻不到頭

NOTES

At first it was very difficult for me to get any sense out of these four verses but at last I got from quite an uncultivated person this explanation which could solve all the difficulties. The words above refer to the theatre and to the actors. In China no female actors are allowed and so the second verse could represent a man who combs the hair as a woman, to act on the stage. It seems furthermore to say in the third verse that although the actors on the stage very often play the part of scholars approved at the examinations yet they have no real reason to be glad there at. The fourth verse then means to say that although loving and affectionates pairs are to be seen on the stage yet that is sham as they are of the same sex. 及第 chi² ti⁴, technical phrase to mean "to be approved at the examinations". 空 k'ung¹, void, vainly. 恩愛 en¹-ai⁴, mutual love derived from gratitude and esteem, as that between husband and wife. 不到頭 pu⁴ tao⁴ t'au², "does not come to a point" that is, has no aim, no regular fruit. as expected after marriage.

TRANSLATION

On a very high mountain there is a high tower (stage) — a man is combing there as a woman — the first candidate approved at the examinations rejoices in vain — and loving husband and wife will never come to a point.

CX

小 元 兒 小 元 兒
偺 們 倆 人 祗 兒
踢 球 打 嘎 兒
上 二 閘 兒
吃 了 一 個 飯 兒
喝 了 一 個 茶 兒
回 到 家 去
偺 們 倆 人 祗 兒

NOTES

小元兒 hsiao³ yüan²'r, " the small First " surname for a boy. 踢 球 t'i¹ ch'iu² to kick balls " sort of game in which the ability consists in pushing with the feet a stone ball and trying to touch the adversary's. 打嘎兒 ta³ ka²'r, another game which consists in throwing very far a wooden ball by mean of a wooden racket called 棒 兒 pang⁴'r. 二 閘 兒 eur¹ cha²'r, the second canal lock near the Tungpien-men. On the banks there is a very elegant resort for young men. Eating-houses provide

meals, female singers, boats and all that is necessary to make a Chinese happy.

TRANSLATION

Small Yüar², small Yüar² — now, let us play —
let us kick the balls or play at rackets — and go to
the second Canal lock — when we shall have taken
a meal — and when we shall have drunk tea — we
will go back home — now, let us play !

CXI

月亮開洗娶不愛燒黑倆隔姜也綠
亮堂開得了存喝鬪餅麬大壁三會靴
爺堂後白個財酒牌麻火錢兒哥過子
門婆媳　花燒個
兒得婦兒　倒有
洗白兒　一
衣白,　大
裳　　落

綠 帽 子
綠 袍 子
綠 套 子

NOTES

月亮爺 yüe¹ liang² ye², " the father moon " name given to the moon by children. 亮堂堂 liang⁴ t'ang¹ t'ang!, very bright. Observe here the change of tone in the word 堂 to be read regularly t'ang². 存財 ts'un² ts'ai², to be economical, to put aside money. 麻花兒 ma² hua¹'r, a sort of bun. — 落 i¹ luo⁴, a pile. These words are supposed to be uttered by a wife who in the night, goes out in the court to wash her linen and working, thinks of her sorrows. 姜三哥 Chiang¹ san¹ ko¹, the word Chiang is a family name. San¹ ko¹, means that the man in question is the third in his family. 過 kuo⁴ is here for 過日子 kuo⁴ jih⁴ tzu, to pass one's life, to live and spend one's days peacefully, that is to say economically and frugally. 綠帽子 lü⁴ mao⁴ tzu, " a green hat; the green colour is in China reserved for deceived husbands, and the phrase " to wear a green hat " means to have a partner in the marriage.

TRANSLATION

The father moon — is so bright ! — I open the back door to wash my linen — I wash it white and I starch it white — but (my husband) after having married me — is thrifty with his money — he likes to drink wine — he likes to play cards — (and likes too) a great pile of cakes and buns — and brown flower biscuits — which cost two big cash each — but here living by us —there is a neighbour, Chiang the third — who knows how to live well — because he has got green boots — and a green hat — and a green garment — and a green jacket.

CXII

兒活了頭襠腳兒兒兒去

寶丫缸褲鍋裏碟面地邊葉裏兒兒去　看穀地　看黃

哴垛養個都禿刷洗刷洗擦洗掃南穀家上

兒草年八的了他裏他裏他裏他到着上

哴上一七好剩讓缸讓鍋讓碟讓崩看再

NOTES

From the beginning of the song I could think that the matter is about a cock, but that is only in a jocose way because afterwards it comes to speak of a girl. 褲襠 k'u⁴ tang⁴, the bottom of the trowsers. 裹脚 kuo¹¹ chiao³. foot-bands used by women with small feet.

TRANSLATION

The cock crowing — has jumped on the heap of grass — every year he bears seven or eight times — the good ones he has all sold — only a bald-headed (small) girl is left — if he lets her wash the vats — she washes there the bottom of the trowsers — if he lets her wash the ricepot — she washes there her footbands — if he lets her wash the saucers — she washes her face in the saucers — if he lets her sweep the ground — she runs away towards the South to look at the grain fields — when she has seen that the grain is yellow — she comes back home.

CXIII

茉 莉 花 兒 丈 夫
茉 莉 花 兒 的 郎
串 枝 蓮 兒 的 枕 頭 綉 海 棠
虞 美 人 兒 姑 娘 走 進 了 房

眼 淚 汪 汪 想 親 娘
臉 擦 官 粉 玫 瑰 露 兒 香
嘴 點 梅 花 胭 脂 玫 瑰 瓣 兒 香
走 一 步 亮 堂 堂
新 買 了 個 小 猪 兒 不 吃 槺
鼓 靠 鼓
鑼 靠 鑼
新 娶 媳 婦 兒 靠 公 婆

NOTES

玫 瑰 露 mei² kuei⁴ lu⁴, rose water; in other cases it means also a sort of white wine. This song seems to be composed of scraps of other songs.

TRANSLATION

The jasmine-husband — the jasmine-bridegroom (is there) — on the wild lotus pillow is embroidered the flower of the *Pyrus spectabilis* — the Rhoeas young-lady enters the room — and weeps bitterly thinking of her own mother — she rubs on her face good cosmetic powder scented with rose water — and she rubs rouge scented like rose petals on her lips — by means of a round cloth shaped like a plum-flower.

CXIV

兒

兒

兒兒 衣

賣兒兒 賣

估錢兒兒刺寺 口糖房 奶皮

宮寺橋廟樓

賣兒烟家根國斗街大家袋奶瓜

弓天字塔袍布跳王蘆牌

下多袋毛扎護大新賣蔣烟王西

大朝大白紅馬三帝湖四

拉是寫是掛是跳是搖是東西底衣抽是兒是賣是安是啃

門就宮就寺就橋就廟就樓就火就灣就寺就口就房就奶

則去天去塔去布去王去牌牌間個去家去國去街去家去奶

平過朝過白過馬過帝過四四間打過毛過護過新過蔣過王

過 去 就 是 火 藥 局
火 藥 局 賣 鋼 針 兒
過 去 就 是 老 城 根 兒
老 城 根 兒 兩 頭 兒 多
過 去 就 是 王 八 窩
晴 天 曬 蓋 子
陰 天 蹚 湯 鍋

NOTES

This song contains a description of the streets in Peking. 平則門 p'ing² tso² men², the central gate in the west-wall of the Manchu city. 拉大弓 la¹ ta⁴ kung¹, to practice archery using a large bow; lit. to draw the long bow. 朝天宮 chao² t'ien¹ kung¹, name of a temple. 白塔寺 pai² t'a³ ssu⁴, the temple of the white pagoda. 掛紅袍 kua⁴ hung² p'ao², to put a red coat on the image of Buddha, as people do who have received a favour. 馬市橋 The horse mart bridge. A bridge on the canal. 搖葫蘆 iao² hu² lu², to shake a gourd, as babies are allowed to do, in order to keep them quiet. 四牌樓 ssu⁴ p'ai³ lou², a square formed by the junction of four streets at right angles. At each side there is a wooden monumental arch. Two of these squares exist in Peking, one in the east of the Tartar city called 東四牌樓 tung¹ ssu⁴ p'ai³ lou² and another in the west of the city called 西四牌樓 hsi¹ ssu⁴ p'ai³ lou², which is alluded to here. 估衣 ku⁴ i¹, old

clothes, the word ku¹ is here pronounced ku⁴. 打火
ta³ huo³, to strike the fire-stone to get fire. Matches
are not yet in general use. 毛家灣 mao² chia² uan¹'r
Mao family's corner-name of place. 扎根刺
cha¹ ken¹ tz'u⁴, to be pricked by a thorn, a needle.
This phrase is merely introduced for the sake of
rhyming with the next verse. 護國寺 hu⁴ kuo² ssu⁴,
temple for the protection of the State. 斗 tou³, a
willow peck, a chinese measure. 新街口 hsin²
chie¹ k'ou³, Mouth of the new street, name of a street.
大糖 ta¹ t'ang², sticks of sugar sold to children. 蔣
家房 chiang³ chia¹ fang², " the house of the Chiang
family " name of street. 安烟袋 an¹ yen¹ tai⁴, to fit
the mouth piece of pipe. In the afore-said street
there is a pipe-shop. 王奶奶 " the old lady
Wang " there is a temple dedicated to her. She
was a very good and religious woman who lived
during the present dynasty and who after her
death was thought to have become a saint spirit,
so that temples were erected to her. 啃 k'en³, to
gnaw; this is naturally purely imaginary as the
good lady had lost all her teeth a very long time
before. 火藥局 huo³ yao⁴ chü², the powder factory.
兩頭兒多 liang² t'ou² r tuo, each part has the same
lenght. 多 is here for 長 ch'ang². 王八窩 uang² pa¹
uo¹, a nest of turtles; this imaginary lair is thought to
give a saucy and witty end to the song. 躥湯鍋
ts'uan¹ t'ang¹ kuo¹, they jump in the broth kettle.
These words are purely absurd.

TRANSLATION

Near the Ping-tso-men they draw long-
bows — next there is the temple Ch'ao-t'ien-
kung — " Ch'ao-t'ien-kung " is written on the
temple in big characters — next there is the
temple of the white Pagoda. — In the white
pagoda people come to give Buddha a red jacket — next there is the Horse mart bridge. — Near
the Horse mart bridge, take three jumps — and
there is the temple of T'i-wang. — near this
temple, shake the gourd — next there are the
four archs. — At the east of the four archs — and
at the west of the four archs — and under the
four archs old clothes are sold — you ask how
much for these old clothes ? — you strike a light
smoke a pipe — you go on and get to the " Corner
of the Mao family ". — Near the corner of the
Mao family one is pricked by a thorn — after that
comes a " temple for the protection of the
State " — near the " temple for the protection of
the State " they sell large willow-pecks — after
that there comes " the mouth of the new street —
near the " mouth of the new street, they sell
sugar sticks — after that is " the house of the
Chiang family — in " the house of the Chiang
family " they fit together smoking pipes — after
that there is the temple of old lady Wang. — Old
lady Wang gnaws the peel of a melon — next
comes the powder factory — near the powder
factory they sell steel needles — after that there

is the wall — the wall is of the same lenght on both sides — after that comes a nest of turtles — in fine weather they warm that shells in the sunshine — and in bad weather they spring in the hoth-pot.

CXV

紫 不 紫
大 海 茄
八 月 裏 供 的 是 兔 兒 爺
自 來 白
自 來 紅
月 光 馬 兒
供 當 中
毛 豆 枝 兒 亂 烘 烘
鷄 冠 子 花 兒 紅 裏 個 紅 靑
圓 月 兒 的 西 瓜 皮 兒 青
月 亮 爺 吃 的 哈 哈 笑
今 夜 的 光 兒 分 外 明

NOTES

The first two verses are the common t'ou²-tzu which has nothing to do with what follows. 海茄 hai³ ch'ie², the egg plant fruit. The Chinese pretend to see in the moon a hare, to which they give offerings on the fifteenth of the 8th moon.

This hare is called 兎兒爺 t'u⁴ r ye². 自來白 tzu⁴ lai² pai², " naturally white " a sort of white cake. 自來紅 tzu⁴ lai² hung², " naturally red " — a cake with sugar on it. 馬兒 ma³ʼr, a picture on which is drawn the moon. Inside the moon the hare is sun piling drugs in a mortar. This picture is burned after the offering. 當中 tang¹ chung¹, in the middle. 毛豆枝兒 soy beans are offered to the rabbit, as this animal is very fond of this food. 亂烘烘 luan⁴ hung¹ hung¹, disorderly irregularly, said of the beans on the branches. 鷄冠子 chi¹ kuan¹ tzu, the cocks comb flower. 紅裏個紅 hung² li³ ko⁴ hung², " red in the red " very red. 圓月兒 yüan² yüe⁴ʼr, like the round moon. The water melon which is called on this occasion 團圓西瓜 t'uan² yüan² hsi¹ kua⁴ (the meeting melon) is cut in as many slices as there are persons in the family.

TRANSLATION

Purple or not purple — the big fruit of the egg-plant ? — In the eighth moon Lord Rabbit is worsh'pped — white cakes — brown cakes — the picture of the moon — is worshipped and played in the middle — the soy beans are in disorder — the cockscomb flowers are of the deepest-red — the peel of the melon offered to the moon is dark — the Lord moon eats and laughs heartily — to-night the moonlight is brighter than usual.

CXVI

說開船就開船
開了船下江南
江南有一個大王廟
大王廟一邊兒一個和尚
一邊兒一個旗杆
今年有一對子戲山
過年跑馬上刀線兒
刀山上有根藍
兩根紅的兩根朝天鐙
男的搬的朝鐙朝天
女的搬的鐙朝天

NOTES.

跑馬 or 跑馬獅的 p'ao3 ma3 hsie4 ti, circus riders. 上刀山 shang1 tao1 shan1, lit. " to climb on the sword mountain " is the name for an exercise seen very often in our circuses; that of jumping from one side of a row of standing swords to the other. 朝天鐙 ch'ao2 t'ien1, teng1, " the staff looking towards the sky " other feat of dexterity which consists in raising one's leg up perpendicularly turning the foot-sole to the sky. 鐙朝天 teng1 ch'ao2 t'ien1, the same phrase as before in a different form.

TRANSLATION

We say " set sail " and the ship starts — the

ship is in motion and we go downwards to Kiang-nan — in Kiang-nan there is a big temple to the great king of heaven — at each side of the Tai-wang-miao there is a priest — and at each side a flagstaff — this year there are a couple of theatrical performances — and next year there will be circusriders and " jumping on the swords " — on the row of swords there are four threads — two of them are red and two are blue — the men perform the feat of " the stirrup looking to the sky — and the women perform the feat of the " stirrup which looks to the sky.

CXVII

```
哥 哥              哭
    三 娘 也 哭    了 哭
車 車 娘 你 別 坐 齊
的 上 娘 娘 三 樹 兒
穀 兒 娘 我 稍 兒
拉 聲 着 麻 鈴 鎈
拉 孩
女 叫
等
芝
掛

想 我 三 娘 一 陣 風
想 我 三 娘 打 門 鐘
莢 藜 開 花 莢 藜 找
誰 想 親 娘 誰 知 道
```

NOTES

拉拉穀 la¹ la¹ ku³, sort of a locust. The begin-

ning of the song is hard to translate. In the second
verse there begins to be light. 三 娘 san¹ niang³,
perhaps it is meant her uncles wife, the uncle being
the third in his family. 坐 齊 了 tsuo¹ ch'i² la, to
sit together, in full number. 芝 麻 稭 兒 樹 chih¹
ma² chie¹'r shu¹, the sesamus plant. This verse
and the following form a sort of 頭 子 in the very
middle of the song, and it is hard to guess why a
bell is spoken of as being attached to that plant.
一 陣 風 i¹ chen⁴ feng¹, my thought goes as quick as
a gust of wind. 打 門 鐘 ta³ men² chung¹, it seems to
me as if I were striking the door-bell. 蒺 藜 花 兒
chi² li² hua¹'r, caltrop flowers.

TRANSLATION

The locust cart and the third brother (?) —
when I, the girl sit down in the cart, my mother
also weeps — I say once : mother, mother do not
weep — wait till the third aunt sits also and then
weep — on the sesamum-tree there hangs a bell —
thinking of my aunt my thought travels as quick
as a guest of wind — thinking of my aunt methinks
I am striking the door-bell at home. — where the
caltrops open their flowers there you may look for
them — only those can understand me who long so
for their mother.

CXVIII

小三兒小三兒
甚麽打拤兒
靑洋汗褟子
白汗褟兒
白汗褟兒鎖着狗牙兒
騎馬穗兒
捧鍋圈兒
靑辮穗兒
緊辮花兒
左邊拔着晚香玉
右邊拔着蒿康尖兒
魚白襪子一道臉兒
雙臉兒鞋一道線兒

NOTES

The toilet of a young lady is here described. 鎖 suo³, to hem clothes, to work a sort of embroidery at the edges of a dress. 狗牙兒 kou³ ya²'r, pattern of embroidery in form of small triangles resembling dog's teeth. 騎馬穗兒 chi² ma³ suei⁴'r, a row of cut hair left standing just before the plaited hair. 捧鍋圈兒 ning² kuo¹ ch'üan¹'r, small braids plaited on children's heads. 辮穗兒 pien⁴ suei¹'r, the silk tassel at the end of a pigtail. 辮花兒 pien⁴ hua¹'r, the knots of a braid. 晚香玉 uan³ hsiang¹ yü⁴, the tuberose. 蒿康尖兒 a shoot of *Ocymum basilicum* (sweet basil). 魚白 yü² pai², as white as a fish skin ; white with a greenish shade of colour. —道臉兒 i¹ tao⁴ lien³⁾ r, " with one surface " this means that no seam is to be seen on the socks. —道線兒 i¹ tao⁴ hsien⁴⁾ r, the two leather strings which come on the shoe are as thin as a thread.

TRANSLATION

Small San'r, small San'r — what dress are you wearing ? — I have got dark crape trowsers — and a white shirt — on the white shirt are embroidered " dog's teeth " — on the head I have a row of standing hair — and some small braids — a dark tassel for my pigtail — and the pigtail is plaited very tight — on the left of my hair I have stuck a tuberose — and on the right a head of sweet basil — I have too white socks with no seam — and my shoes have leather strings as thin as a thread.

CXIX

隔着牆兒扔切糕
撅兒豆兒都掉了
隔着牆兒扔磚頭
砸了妞兒的兩把兒頭
隔着牆兒扔桼子
怎麼知道姑娘沒落子

NOTES

I do not think that this song can be properly understood by children, but the fact is that numbers of them sing these verses the meaning of which is rather equivocal. It alludes to a man who tries to win a young girl in different comical ways. 切 糕 ch'ie¹ kao¹, slices of pudding made with flower, dates and leng beans. 兩 把 兒 頭 liang³ pa¹ʼ r t'ou³, "a head with two handles" chinese name for the manchu women's head-gear. This leads one to suppose that this rhyme originated from bannermen. 沒 落 子 mei² lao¹ tzu, means literally has not a halting-place, a refuge-and then, to be in a miserable condition, to be poor, not to know where to go.

TRANSLATION

From outside the wall he throws slices of pudding — the dates and the long beans all fell to the ground. — From outside the wall he throws lumps of bricks — and has broken the girl's manchu head-gear — from outside the wall he throws bank-notes — how does he know that the girl has no means ?

CXX

廟 裏 的 和 尚 拉 大 鎖
挨 家 兒 搖 鈴 鐺

廟
了
賣兒
覺
杆
打磬

米旗不攤着頂
月了全小生不姑大念香不盡髮行
化聲典道尚落睡大拿怎麼燒茶頭不修
尚十尚袍攔花不姑大麼香打留頭行
和嘆的魚和的隔壁和於和兒的
的兒的勒的抓的脖的噹的字兒
裏家裏裏把裏着了裏兒裏裏個
廟挨廟摩廟大廟想跪廟叮廟一

NOTES

This song is one of the less devotional towards the buddhist priests and is widely sung in Peking by children and grown people. 大鎖 ta[1] suo[3], a large chain which the priests fasten to their neck and drag around when travelling about to collect alms. Sometimes, in order to excite pity and devotion, this chain is made so heavy that the help of a second man is required to drag it along. 挨家兒 ai[2] chia[1]' r, from one house to the other in succession. 化月米 hua[4] yüe[4] mi[3], to collect the monthly rice. Many families are in the habit of giving every month a quantity of rice to certain temples. The first and fifteenth of the month a priest goes around with a coolie who bears a barril to collect the offerings. 摩 勒 魚 兒 muo² lo¹ yü²' r, a wooden drum in the shape of a fish'head; this instrument is beaten during the ceremonies, and is also taken round by almsbegging priests who carry it on their back tied by a cord. 道 袍 tao⁴ p'ao², the priests ceremonial dress. 落 花 生 luo⁴ hua¹ sheng¹, ground nuts. 拿 大 頂 na² ta⁴ ting³, to stand on one's head, as jugglers do. 磬 ch'ing⁴, a copper instrument struck during a religious service. — 個 字 兒 i¹ ko⁴ tzu⁴' r, "in one word" altogether, with no exception. 修 行 hsiu¹ hsing², to perfect and reform one's character, as chinese priests are supposed to do in their temples.

TRANSLATION

The priest of the temple drags a heavy chain — and goes from one house to the other ringing a bell — the priest of the temple goes out for the monthly rice — and from house to house he sighs ten times, — the priest in the temple has mortgaged the flag-staffs and has sold the temple — and he does not want either the fish-drum or the ceremonial dress — the priest in the temple has prepared a small fruit stall — (and says) " ground nuts, a big handful of them ! — The priest in the temple cannot sleep — because he is thinking of the neighbour's elder daughter — the priest in the temple stands on his head — but

having sprained his neck how could he read the
sacred books? — The priest in the temple does
not strike the copperdrum — but ding dong! he
strikes instead the tea-cup — the priest in the
temple lets his hair grow — and does not care a
bit about the improvement of his moral conduct.

CXXI

膠 泥 瓣 兒
使 勁 兒 摔
刻 了 爺 爺 兒
刻 奶 奶 兒
爺 爺 兒 戴 着 一 頂 困 秋 帕
奶 奶 兒 戴 着 一 枝 鳳 頭 釵

NOTES

This song is sung by children who play at
making mud-pies. 膠 泥 chiao¹ ni², the clay mixed
up with water becomes sticky like glue. 泥 瓣 兒
ni² pan⁴' r, a block of clay. 使 勁 摔 shih³ ching⁴' r
shuai¹, cast it with force on the ground. Before
the clay is fit to be put into the moulds, it must be
rendered softer and that result is obtained by
beating the clay repeatedly on the ground. 刻,
read here k'o¹ and not k'o⁴, to mould. The moulds
sold to the boys in the streets are of different
forms and some of them have the form of a man or

of a woman. 困 秋 帽 k'un⁴ c'iu¹ mao⁴, an old round hat. 鳳 頭 釵 feng¹ t'ou² ch'ai¹, a hair-pin for women; it means literally a phoenix-head pin.

TRANSLATION

The sticky clay blocks — first we throw them on the ground, and then we mould out a gentleman — we mould out a lady — the gentleman wears on old round hat — and the lady a phoenix-head hairpin.

CXXII

祭 竈 祭 竈 新 年 來 到
老 頭 子 過 來 要 毡 帽
老 婆 子 過 來 要 裹 脚
小 淘 氣 兒 過 來 要 花 炮

NOTES

These words are pronounced while sacrificing to the god of the stoves near the end of the year. 裹 脚 kuo³ chiao³, ankle bands for ladies trowsers. At the New-year and the days which precede it, every body tries to dress well and to look his best. 小 淘 氣 兒 hsiao³ t'ao² ch'i⁴r, general nickname given to children meaning the small impertinent. 花 炮 hua¹ p'ao⁴, crackers.

TRANSLATION

Sacrifice to the god of the stoves, Sacrifice to the god of the stoves, the new-year has arrived — the old man comes over and wants a felt-hat — the old lady comes over and wants anklebands — the impertinent youngster comes over and wants crackers.

CXXIII

滴滴滴
上草垛
他媽養活獨一個
金盆洗
銀盆臥
一聘聘到山東克
十個公
十個婆
十個小叔子管着我
叫他井台兒去打水
勒的小手兒怪疼得
樹上鳥
歧兒扎的叫
受苦受難誰知道

NOTES

滴滴滴 ti¹ ti¹ ti¹, imitates the noise made by

a chicken. 克 k'o⁴, an unusual pronunciation of the word 去 ch'ü⁴, to go. It is specially used by bannermen and old fashioned people. 小叔子 hsiao³ shu² tzŭ, husband's younger brothers. 井台 兒 ching³ t'ai²' r, the well step. 勒手 lei⁴ shou³ " to have one's hands strangled " that is to say to hurt one's hands by pulling with a rope. 吱兒扎 chih¹'r cha₁, is supposed to imitate the birds chattering. 難 nan⁴, in the fourth tone, means adversity, trouble.

TRANSLATION

The chicken screaming — flies on the grass-stack. — Her mother had reased only her — she washed in a gold basin — she slept in a silver basin — and then they married her in the Shan-tung — (it looks as if she had) ten fathers-in-law — and ten mothers-in-law — and ten brothers-in-law to watch her — now they let her go to the well to draw water — and her small hands are swollen with the great pain — the birds on the trees — chatter merrily — who knows that I am suffering bitterness and pain ?.

CXXIV

月 亮 爺
亮 堂 堂
街 坊 的 姑 娘 要 嫁 粧

錠兒粉
棒兒香
棉花胭脂二百張

NOTES

錠兒粉 ting⁴'r fen³, an inferior quality of cosmetic powder in square pieces. 棒兒香 pang⁴'r hsiang¹, an incense stick. 棉花胭脂 mien² hua¹ yen¹ chih¹, small cotton strip of cloth imbued with cosmetic rouge, to paint women's lips.

TRANSLATION

The father-moon — is bright and shining — the neighbour's girl wants her bridal presents — squares of cosmetic powder — incense sticks — and two hundred rouge cotton-strips.

CXXV

松枝兒樹
掛鈴鐺
親娘賣我在小船兒上
糉子米飯
小魚兒湯
端起飯碗兒想親娘
擱下飯碗兒上後艙
哭了一聲哥哥妹妹誰還想誰

親娘想我一陣風
我想親娘在夢中

NOTES

The first two verses form the common introduction. The word 松枝兒樹 sung¹ chib¹ʳ shu⁴, means literally a fir-branched tree, that is the same as 松樹 sung¹ shu⁴, a fir-tree. 糉子米 suo¹-tzǔ mi³, a coarse quality of rice; the character is not to be found in any dictionary, but is currently written as above. The words are supposed to be uttered by a small boy who has been sold by his mother to be a small servant on a boat. 一陣風 i¹ chen⁴ feng¹, here, as quick as a gale of wind.

TRANSLATION

On the fir-tree — there is a small bell — my own mother has sold me on board a boat — (I eat here) course rice — and fish broth — taking the rice-bowl to my mouth I think of my mother — when I lay down the rice-bowl then I go to the stern rooms — and I shed some tears saying: brothers, sisters, which of us thinks of each other? — the care of my mother for me has been as fleeting as a squall of wind — but I think of my mother in my dreams.

CXXVI

黃豆粒兒圓上圓，
養活了丫頭不值錢，
值二塊豆腐二兩酒。
送在婆婆家大門口，
婆婆說脚大也罷臉又醜也罷，
公公說留着他燒茶炙飯。

NOTES

黃豆 huang[2] tou[4], a small sort of yellow haricot (*Phaseolus flavus*). 圓上圓 yüan[2] shang[4] yüan[2], "round on round" that means very much round. The song is taken from the country and that may be observed in some phrases different from the pure Pekinese. For instance the last verse says: 燒茶炙飯 shao[1] ch'a[2] chu[3] fan[4], instead of 沏茶炙飯 ch'i[1] ch'a[2] chu[3] fan[4], to prepare tea and food.

TRANSLATION

The yellow haricot — is completely round — bearing a daughter, she is worth no money — just as much as two bits of bean-curd and two ounces of wine. — when we send her to her mother-in-law's house — the mother-in-law says: her feet are large and her face is ugly — the father-in-law says : let her stay, let her stay ! — she can be use-ful for boiling tea and cooking food.

CXXVII

松 栢 枝 兒

碾 子 軋

我 跟 姐 姐 同 出 嫁

姐 姐 嫁 在 南 山 裏

妹 妹 嫁 在 比 窪 裏

NOTES

栢 樹 pai³ shu⁴, the cypress. The branches of fir and cypress are burned in some offerings to the spirits, but here the second verse has no rational meaning.

TRANSLATION

The branches of fir and cypress — are crushed by a stone roller (?) — I and my elder sister both marry — my elder sister will marry in the mountains of the South — and I will marry in the Northern bogs.

CXXVIII

一 個 毽 兒

拍　兩　辦　兒
打　花　鼓　兒
繞　花　線　兒
裏　拐　外　拐
八　仙　過　海
九　十　九　個　一　百

NOTES

The shuttle-cok is kicked by boys but the girls push the ball with their hands and this is called 拍 p'ai¹. Sometimes while playing they sing some rhymes, one of which I present to the reader. 拍 兩 辦 兒 p'ai¹ liang³ pan''ɪ r, is struck so hard as to be broken in two pieces. 打 花 鼓 兒 ta³ hua¹ ku³, sort of musical amusement consisting of a song accompanied by drum beating performed generally by girls. This drum beating is accompanied by various evolutions of the arms, non unlike the movement of pushing the shuttle-cok. — 繞 花 線 兒 jao⁴ hua¹ hsien⁴, r, another game. The player places the shuttle-cok on his foot, kicks it in the air, awaits its falling down, and just before it touches the ground, he turnes the foot down round it and kicks it up again. 裏 拐 外 拐 liu³ kai³ uai⁴ kuai³, pushing inside and pushing outside the shuttle-cok.

TRANSLATION

A shuttle-cok — is kicked up and broken in

two pieces — beat the drum — pick up the shuttle-cock. — push inside, push outside — the eight genii cross the sea — ninety nine and a hundred.

———————

CXXIX

門兒敲得梆梆
狗兒咬得汪汪
我說一聲誰
騎着毛驢兒
扛着米
要粗的
要細的
量糠兒的
簸净兒的

NOTES

梆梆 pang1 pang1, imitates the knock at the door. 汪汪 uang1 uang1, the barking of a dog. 毛驢兒 mao2 lü2, r, a common name for an ass, instead of the simple 驢兒 lü2' r. A slang word for it is 毛團兒 mao2' t'uan2' r; here the rice-seller is supposed to advertise his wares in the last four verses. 量糠兒的 liang2 k'ang1 'r ti2, rice and husks together, rice which has not been winnowed. 簸净兒的 puo3 ching4' r ti, clean rice with no husks.

TRANSLATION

People knock at the door — and the dog
barks — I ask once, who is there? — (the rice
seller) rides an ass — and bears the rice on his
back. — (he says) do you want coarse rice? — do
you want fine rice? — here is rice and husk, —
and here is winnowed rice.

CXXX

小 陶 氣 兒
跳 鑽 鑽 兒
腦 瓜 兒 上 梳 着 個 小 蠟 千 兒
一 入 學 了 八 宗 藝
撞 鐘 踢 球 外 帶 打 嘎

NOTES

跳 鑽 鑽 兒 t'iao⁴ tsuan¹ tsuan¹ʳ r, hopping and
jumping. 蠟 千 兒 la⁴ c'ien¹ʳ r, a chinese candlestick.
When boys have not yet hair enough to comb a
pigtail, sometimes their hair is bound up in a small
plait which stands perpendicularly on the top of
the head. 八 宗 藝 pa¹ tsung² i⁴, eight kinds of
abilities. 撞 鐘 chuang⁴ chung⁴, lit. "to strike the
bell". A game practised by boys who each throw
a piece of cash against a wall. The greater or
lesser distance to which the cash rebounds from

the wall makes one the winner or loser. 外帶 uai⁴ tai⁴, and furthermore.

TRANSLATION

The impertinent youngster — goes hopping and jumping — he has a " candle " toupet on his head — he himself has mastered eight sorts of abilities — he can play at " bell-striking " at foot-ball and also at wood ball.

CXXXI

打 羅 兒 篩
曳 羅 兒 篩
該 我 的 麪 錢 不 拿 來
多 會 兒 拿 來
逛 燈 拿 來
甚 麼 燈
小 脚 兒 燈
一 登 登 了 個 大 窟 窿

NOTES

逛燈 kuang⁴ teng¹, a festival from the 13ᵗʰ to the 17ᵗʰ of the first moon. In the evening lanterns are hung out by shops and private houses. 小脚兒燈 hsiao³ chiao³⁾ r teng¹. A lantern shaped in the form of a chinese small foot. The introduction to this song is identical with another translated before. 燈 is pronounced like "lantern" therefore the pun.

TRANSLATION

Strike the sieve and sift — drag the sieve and sift — you owe me money for flour and do not pay me — when will you bring it here? — At the festival of Lanterns I'll bring it — what lantern? — The small foot lantern. — walking on it I made a big hole in it.

CXXXII

小　大　姐
繞　十　八
滿　臉　的　鋸　子　大　疤　拉
桃　兒　粉
任　意　兒　搽
胭　脂　抹　的　血　絲　胡　拉
梳　着　一　個　蘇　州　纂　兒
鬢　角　兒　斜　插　一　枝　花
金　蓮　多　麼　大
橫　量　二　寸　八

NOTES

小大姐 hsiao³ ta¹ chie³, the young lady. The picture is humourous. 鋸子 chü¹ tzu, "a saw" it refers to the fact that after the small pox the skin of the face sometimes is glued together thus forming a scar and a small pimple on it. 桃兒粉 t'ao²'r fen³, red cosmetic powder sold in peach like beads. 血絲胡拉, read almost in one word hsie³ sz-hu-là. I have only adopted these characters in order to write down the sound as spoken; the general meaning is to look as if besmeared with blood — 橫量 heng² liang², measuring the size of the foot. The smallest foot is three inches.

TRANSLATION

The young lady — has just reached her eighteenth year — she has the face full of pimples and scars — with red cosmetic — she rubs all over the face to her heart's desire and then she combs her hair into a Soo-chow chignon — near the temple she sticks a flower in her hair — how big is her foot? — altogether two inches and eight tenths of an inch.

CXXXIII

我 的 兒
我 的 姣
三 年 不 見 長 的 這 麼 高
騎 着 我 的 馬
拿 着 我 的 刀
扛 着 我 的 案 板 賣 切 糕

TRANSLATION

My son — my treasure — during the three
years that I have not seen you, you have grown so
tall — riding my horse — taking my swoard —
bearing on your shoulder my kneading-board and
selling slices of pudding.

CXXXIV

豆 芽 菜
水 溯 溯
誰 家 的 媳 婦 兒 打 公 公
公 公 拿 着 柺 棍 兒 拐
媳 婦 兒 拿 着 袖 口 兒 甩

NOTES

豆芽菜 tou¹ ya² ts'ai⁴, bean sprouts commonly
eaten in China. 水澎澎 shuei³ p'eng¹ p'eng¹, flowing
with water; these sprouts are put in water to keep
them fresh.

TRANSLATION

The bean sprouts — are dripping with water
— who is the wife who dares to beat her father in
law? — the father-in-law beats her with his stick
— and the woman only lets her sleeve down (with
anger).

CXXXV

秦始皇
皇牆兒窄

始城頭兒着來里着了塌了

秦砌牆磴擋後千對哭哭

矮
子個尋一聲半

過孟夫哭天邊兒

不姜

來女兒

NOTES

秦始皇 ch'in2 shih3 huang2, the emperor who built the great wall and who is said to have had buried in it all the men who died during its building. 城墻 ch'eng2 ch'iang2 "the fortified wall" the full name is 萬里長城 uan3 li3 ch'ang2 ch'eng2. 磴兒窄 teng4'r chai3, the layers of brick are so thin that a man is able to creep on the wall as up stairs. 孟姜女 Meng4 chiang3 nü3. A beautiful woman whose husband, although a hsiu4 ts'ai2, was forced to work at the wall; being in delicate health he died and was buried in the brickwork. When his wife came for him and heard of his end, she knelt by the wall and wept invoking Heaven. She so moved Heaven that the wall crumbled away at the spot and showed her husband's remains: she piously exhumed them, and took them with her. She was afterwards rewarded by the Emperor who granted her a precious belt. But she was so oppressed with grief that at last she ran her head against a wall and died.

TRANSLATION

The Emperor Shih-huang — built the Great Wall — the top of the wall was low — and the steps were short — to prevent the Tartars from crossing — There was Meng chiang nü — who came from a thousand miles away to find her husband — then wept in front of the wall — wept and cried : O Heaven ! — and at her tears the side of the wall fell down.

CXXXVI

換 個 牛
牛 沒 甲
換 匹 馬
馬 沒 鞍
上 南 山
南 山 一 窩 兔 兒
剝 了 皮 兒 绑 條 裤 兒

跤 跤 蹺
換 把 刀
刀 不 快
切 青 菜
菜 兒 青
換 把 弓
弓 沒 頭

NOTES

This rhyme has no sense all through. 跤 蹺 hsi[1] ch'iao[1], extraordinary, uncommon ; at least it is the only meaning and writing which may reasonably agree with the pronunciation **hsi¹ ch'iao⁴**.

TRANSLATION

Very extraordinary — change a sword — the sword does not cut — hash vegetables — their leaves are green — change a bow — the bow has no head — change an ox — the ox has no scales — change a horse — the horse has no saddle — go to the South hills — in the southern hills there is a nest of hares — from which we take the skin to make a pair of trowsers.

CXXXVII

白 塔 寺
有 白 塔
塔 上 有 磚 沒 有 瓦
塔 臺 兒 上 裂 了 一 道 縫
魯 班 爺 下 來 鋸 上 塔

NOTES

Near the P'ing-tso-men there is a pagoda already spoken of in rhyme N°114. During this dynasty it threatened to collapse and showed a great crack. The popular tradition says that just at that time somebody dressed like a mason walked round and round the place shouting the words. 鋸 大 傢 伙 兒 **chü¹ ta⁴ chia¹ huo⁵ r** " mend the big thing ". A few days after, with great astonishment the candid Pekinese observed that the crack in the pagoda had been repaired and on the fresh work was visible the mark of a mason's trowel. The popular fancy nowhere so wildly developed as in China, directly connected this mysterious piece of masonry with the workman's words and recognized in him Lu³ pan¹ ye², the Genius protector of masons and carpenters. As to the historical truth of the work so well executed, it may be explained in two ways : either the work had been done by government order and at an uncommon time of the day : or more probably that crack had never existed.

TRANSLATION

At the temple of Pai-t'a-ssu, there is a white pagoda — on the pagoda there are bricks but not tiles — on the pagoda's pedestal a gaping crack appeared — and Lu-pan-ye himself came down to repair it.

CXXXVIII

麻 子 鬼
偷 涼 水
搬 倒 了 缸
砸 了 腿
你 賠 我 的 缸
我 賠 你 的 腿

NOTES

瘡子兒 ma² tzu kuei¹, is said jocularly about a child much marked by smallpox.

TRANSLATION

The " small pox devil " — stealing the water — has upset the bucket — and has broken his leg — you repay me for my bucket — and I will repay you for your leg.

CXXXIX

喜 花 榴 來 戴 滿 頭
喜 酒 兒 斟 上 嘔 幾 嘔
喜 鳥 兒 落 在 房 簷 兒 上
哨 的 是 喜 報 三 元 獨 占 鰲 頭

NOTES

The hsi³ or joy here alluded, to is the approval at the examinations. 嘔 ou¹, means to drink, to gulp down. 三 元 san¹ yüan²: a candidate who has taken the highest places at the examinations. These words are pronounced by the joy-messengers 報喜的 pao⁴ hsi³ ti, when they reach the door of the successful candidate. 獨占鰲頭 tu² chan⁴ ao¹ t'ou², (the man who has been successful at the last Hanlin examinations is said) to have alone occupied the Ao-fish's head.

TRANSLATION

Here are the flowers of joy, pick them up and cover your head with them — here is the wine of joy, pour it out and drink — the birds of joy come to stop under the eaves of the roof — and the news they bear is : the first successful candidate at the examinations.

CXXXX

錐 幫 子 兒
納 底 子 兒
掙 了 二 升 小 米 子 兒
蒸 蒸 烙 烙
吃 他 娘 的 一 頓 犒 勞

NOTES

This rhyme speaks jocularly of a little fellow who is supposed to work in order to give himself a treat. 小米 hsiao³ mi³, millet — 蒸 cheng¹, to steam. 烙 lao⁴, to fry in a pan. 犒勞 k'ao⁴ lao², a treat given on some lucky days, to soldiers or workmen.

TRANSLATION

(The boy) bores the heelband of the shoe — and stitches the shoe sole — he has earned two pecks of millet — after a good deal of steaming and frying — he eates a good meal given to him by his mother as a reward.

CXXXXI

月 亮 爺
明 煌 煌
騎 着 大 馬 去 燒 香
大 馬 拴 在 梧 桐 樹
小 馬 拴 在 廟 門 兒 上

NOTES

明 煌 煌 ming² huang² huang², extremely bright.
梧 桐 u² t'ung², the *Sterculia platanifolia* (Catalpa).

TRANSLATION

The Lord moon — how bright he is — on horse-back I go to burn incense — the big horse is bound to the Catalpa tree — and the small horse to the temple door.

CXXXXII

高 高 山 上 一 窩 猪
兩 口 于 打 架 孩 于 哭
孩 于 孩 子 你 別 哭
等 着 我 打 那 個 老 丈 夫

NOTES

The first verse is a good sample of those extraordinary introductions.

TRANSLATION

On a very high mountain there is a lair of pigs — a husband and a wife quarrel and the child weeps — child, child, do not weep — wait till I thrash this old husband.

CXXXXIII

廟 門 兒 對 廟 門 兒
裏 頭 住 着 個 小 娅 人 兒
白 臉 蛋 兒
紅 嘴 唇 兒
扭 扭 搗 搗 愛 死 個 人 兒

NOTES

扭 扭 搗 搗 niu³ niu³ nie⁴ nie⁴, to walk in a sweet and graceful manner.

TRANSLATION

A door of the temple is opposite to a door of the temple — there lives a small girl — with white cheeks — and red lips — she walks so nicely that she makes people die of love.

CXXXXIV

高　鳥　鳥　鳥
　　兒　量　身
　　飯　吃　要
　　腰　毛　先

架　打　要
抄　手　用
臉　洗　要
澆　水　拿

NOTES

鳥, read here **niao¹** and not **niao³** — the word has no sense and is purely phonetical. 毛腰 **mao² yao¹**, the person spoken of being so tall, must stoop down to take his food. 抄 **ch'ao¹** (written some times when in this sense with another vulgar character) means here to lift up somebody by catching him under the armpits. 澆 **chiao**, to water, to poor down water.

TRANSLATION

Hallo! — he is really tall — when he wants to eat — he must stoop down — when he wants to fight — he lifts his adversary under the arms — when he wants to wash his face — he poures water down on it (rather than to stop down to the basin).

CXXXXV

這 個 人 生 來 性 兒 急
清 晨 早 起 去 趕 集

錯 穿 了 綠 布 褲
倒 騎 着 一 頭 驢

NOTES

綠 布 褲 lü⁴ pu⁴ k'u⁴, trowsers made of green cloth, trowsers for a woman. The man in his haste had put on his wife's trowsers. 倒 騎 tao⁴ ch'i², to ride with the head turned to the animal's tail.

TRANSLATION

This man is very hasty by nature — early in the morning he started for the fair — and he had put on by mistake his wife's trowsers — and was riding with his head towards the donkey's tail.

CXLVI

窮 太 太 兒
抱 着 個 肩 兒
吃 完 了 飯 兒
遛 了 個 灣 兒
又 買 檳 榔
又 買 烟 兒

TRANSLATION

The poor woman — folds her arms on her

12

breast — when she has finished taking her food —
she goes out for a strall — and buys betelnuts —
and tobacco.

CXLVII

是　誰　拍　我　的　門　兒
小　狗　兒　汪　汪　叫
親　家　太　太　來　到　了
忙　着　穿　花　鞋
褲　腿　兒　又　掉　了

TRANSLATION

Who knocks at the door ? — the small dog
barks — a lady relation has arrived — in a hurry
I put on my embroidered shoes — but my
anklebands have fallen down.

CXLVIII

大　哥　哥，二　哥　哥，
這　個　年　頭　兒　怎　麼　過
棒　子　麵　兒　二　百　多
扁　豆　開　花　兒　一　呀　兒　喲

NOTES

年頭 nien² t'ou², the crops of the year. 怎麼
過 tsen³ mo kuo¹, how will it be possible to live? 棒
子麵 pang¹-tzu-mien¹ flour of Indian corn. 二百多
eur¹ pai³ tuo¹, more than two pai for a chin₁, a chinese
pound. The last verse has no sense and ends the
rhyme as the person tries to divert the attention
to another subject.

TRANSLATION

First elder brother — second elder brother —
with these crops how will it be possible to live? —
Indian corn flour is sold at two cents a pound! —
the bean plant opens its flowers, Hallo!

CXLIX

正 月 裏 正 月 正
七 個 老 西 兒 去 逛 燈
反 穿 皮 襖 還 嫌 冷
河 裏 的 王 老 八 他 怎 麼 過 冬

NOTES

反穿皮襖 fan³ ch'uan¹ p'i² ao², wearing the fur
coat with the fur outside, to feel warmer. Here the
words are said to have a laugh at the Shan-hsi
men. 王老八 uang² lao³ pa¹ is instead of 老王八,
the old turtle.

TRANSLATION

In the first month, in the first month — seven Shan-hsi people go out in the streets to see the lanterns. — they wear their furs outside and yet they feel cold — but look at the turtles in the river, how do they manage to live through the winter?

CL

小 小 子 兒 開 鋪 兒
開 開 鋪 兒 兩 扇 門 兒
小 棹 子 兒
小 椅 子 兒
烏 木 筷 子 兒 小 碟 子 兒

NOTES

烏 木 u⁴ mu⁴, ebony wood.

TRANSLATION

The small boy has opened a shop — he has opened a shop with two front doors — with small tables — and small chairs — and chop-sticks of ebony wood.

CLI

小 姑 娘 作 一 夢
夢 見 婆 婆 來 下 定

箕 金 條
裏 金 條
扎 花 兒 裙 子 綉 花 兒 襖

NOTES

下定 hsia⁴ ting⁴, the future mother-in-law goes to the bride's parents and presents the bridal gifts. After this ceremony the marriage is considered fixed and the girl cannot on any account be betrothed to another man. 金條 chin¹ t'iao², short golden rods sold in the gold-shops called 金店 chin¹ tien⁴. Each rod may weigh generally from one to four chinese ounces (liang). 裏金條 kuo³ chin¹ t'iao², sham gold rods given sometimes as gifts.

TRANSLATION

The small girl — has had a dream — she has dreamt of her mother-in-law coming to give her the bridal gift — real gold rods — and sham gold rods — a gown with stitched flowers — and a cloak with embroidered flowers.

CLII

養 活 猫 吃 口 肉
養 活 狗 會 看 家
養 活 貓 會 拏 耗 子
養 活 你 這 丫 頭 作 甚 麼

NOTES

These words are playfully said by parents to their small daughters. — 口 肉 i¹ k'ou³ jou⁴, a mouthful of meat, some meat.

TRANSLATION

If we keep a pig — it is in order to enjoy a good piece of meat — if we keep a dog — it is in order to have him watch the house — if we keep a cat — it is to have him eat the mice — but to keep a maid like you — what is the use of it?

CLIII

喜 兒 喜 兒　　賠 了 本 兒
賣 涼 粉 兒　　娶 了 個 媳 婦 兒
砸 了 鑵 子　　一 條 腿 兒

NOTES

喜 兒 hsi³ 'r, may be shortened from 喜 雀 hsi³ ch'iao³, a magpie, but here it is used as a common nickname for children, meaning "joy". 涼 粉 兒 liang² fen³ 'r, fresh powder, is white bean-flour which in summer time is kept by merchants in an ice-box to sell it cool. 鑵 子 kiuan⁴ tzü³, a pot taken around by the bean-flour sellers, in which they keep a sort of sauce to season their ware before selling it to customers.

一 條 腿 兒 i¹ t'iao² t'uei³'r, (with) one leg. It must however be noticed that this phrase also means in Pekinese language " very harmoniously, very peacefully" when speaking of a loving husband and wife : as the two persons were only one, tied one to the other, having one leg in two and therefore with one will and wish.

TRANSLATION

Joy, Joy — sells cool bean-flour — but he has broken the sauce jar — and has forfeited his capital — now he has married a wife — with one leg (or, and he is very happy with her).

CLIV

鼓 靠 着 鼓 來
鑼 靠 鑼
新 娶 的 媳 婦 兒 靠 公 婆
月 亮 爺 靠 着 娑 羅 兒 樹
牛 郎 織 女 緊 靠 天 河

NOTES

These first verses refer to the ceremonies of a marriage procession, so often mentioned before. — According to chinese folk-lore it is related that in the moon there is a big tree called

娑 羅 兒 樹 suo¹ luo²ʳ r shu¹ (*Shorea robusta*) on which the father moon leans. The word *solo* is derived from the sanscrit sâla. In the first two verses the word k'ao, to recline, to lean, is used in the sense of to be contiguous, near, in great number. 牛 郎 niu² lang² or also 牽 牛 ch'ien¹ niu², the constellation of the Herdboy. 織女 chih¹ nü³, the Spinning damsel, another constellation. The former and the latter are placed each at one side of the milky way ; the Chinese consider them to be husband and wife and say that once a year they succeed in seeing each other by a curious expedient. The magpies form themselves into a bridge over the milky way (天 河 t'ien¹ ho²) and the pair get on the bridge and meet. Many particulars are related about this annual interview ; there is also a fantastical play called 渡 銀 河 tu⁴ yin² ho², the " Crossing of the silver river " in which the adventures and sorrows of this loving pair are exposed to mortal eyes.

TRANSLATION

(In the marriage procession) drums succeed drums — and gongs succeed gongs — a newly married bride relies on her father and mother-in-law — the father moon reclines on the Shorea tree — and the constellations of the Herdboy and the Spinning damsel each lie on one side of the milky way.

CLV

紅	得	哩		七	根	鬚 兒
指	甲	草 兒		六	個	瓣 兒
藍	得	哩		晚	香	玉 得 哩
翠	雀	兒		矮	康	尖 兒

NOTES

Pekinese boys sing these words to imitate the street-call of the flower sellers. The two sounds which I have written 得 哩 to-li, and occur three times in these verses are altogether phonetic and with no meaning tone or accent; so the first verse is pronounced as if it were written hung toli. 指 甲 草 兒 chih³ chia³ ts'ao³ʳ r (pronounce chih² chia³) lit. finger grass, is the China balsam (*Impatiens balsamina*) with whose red flowers chinese ladies dye their fingers, as the Arab women with the hennè. The flowers of this plant may have different shades of colour from plain white to deep red, and are also called 鳳 仙 花 feng⁴ hsien¹ hua¹. 翠 雀 兒 ts'uei¹ ch'iao³ʳ r, the larkspur. 花 鬚 兒 hua¹ hsü¹ʳ r, stamens and style of flowers. 矮 康 ai¹ k'ang¹, an aromatic plant, basilic (*Ocimum basilicum*),

TRANSLATION

Here is the red ! — China balsam — here is the blue ! — the larkspur — with seven stamens — and six petals — the tuberose — and the basilic grass.

CLVI

大娘二娘猜
三娘罵我醜奴才的
我也不是偷來的
我也不是跑來的
花紅綠轎兒娶來的
瞧瞧奴家的手
金珠瑪瑙一大斗
瞧瞧奴家的牙
從小兒愛喝個菓子茶

NOTES

It happens very often in a family that all the brothers marry and do not live in seperate establishments. All the young wives live together and in order to distinguish them, the elder brother's wife is called ta¹-niang², the second brother's eur¹ niang² and so forth. In this way a system of subordination prevails in the family, and the older wives indulge rather often in teasing the younger ones, The ta¹-niang², this powerful chief of this female clan has a greater authority than all and is consequently allowed to brew the most mischief possible in the family. 猜 ts'ai¹, lit. to guess, to solve riddles, very probably means here to guess, to doubt, to make investigations, suppositions on the woman who is the plaintiff in the song, the youngest wife who complains of having been insulted. 醜 奴 才 ch'ou³ nu² ts'ai² " ugly slave " a must insulting appellation to a woman who has been legally married, implying that she is not a legal wife but a bought slave. 偷 來 的 t'ou₁ lai₂ ti, to come stealthily, that is to say come and live with a man without any legal and customary sanction. The same meaning is very curiously expressed in the phrase 手 拉 手 兒 來 的 shou³ la¹ shou³ lai² ti — lit. "to come taking each other by the hand" that is said of two persons who like each other and without parental permission and the ordinary ceremony take each other by the hand and go and live together. — After that in English would be found " but "; this most interesting particle is wanting here. 花 紅 轎 hua¹ hung² chiao¹, " the chair as red as (red) flowers, in which the bride sits, when she is taken from her own paternal house to her husband's. 綠 轎 lü¹ chiao¹, one or two green chairs in which sit some of the girl's relations to take her to the new home. 奴 家 nu² chia¹, a term of modesty used by wives for " I " — 瑪 瑙 ma¹ nao³, cornelion. 菓 子 茶 kuo³ tzu ch'a², " tea with sugared fruits, as taken by rich people.

TRANSLATION

The first wife and the second wife play at guissing riddles — the third wife insults me as " an ugly slave" — but I did not come here stealthily — nor did I run away to come here — I was married and taken here in a red chair and was followed by green chairs — look here at my hands ! — I could fill a big peck with the gold pearls and cornelion that I wear — look here at my teeth! — since I was a child I have been accustomed to take " tea with candied fruits ".

CLVII

小 胖 小 子 兒 眞 有 哏 兒
你 可 愛 死 個 人 兒
小 胖 小 子 兒 胖 達 達
你 是 誰 家 的 愛 娃 娃
買 美 人 兒
買 美 人 兒
買 到 家 裏 作 個 看 家 的 人 兒
有 人 兒
沒 人 兒
不 用 鎖 門 兒

NOTES

哏 兒 ken²ʳ r, no recognized character exists

for this word which means, amusing, pleasant. These words are from a mother to her own boy. — 愛死 ai⁴ ssŭ³, to cause somebody to die of love. 胖達達 p'ang⁴ ta¹ ta¹, very fat and big; observe here ta¹ for ta². 愛娃娃 ai⁴ ua² ua², a beloved child. 美人兒 mei³³ jen²⁰ r, a beauty, said particularly of women, but here of the boy.

TRANSLATION

This fat boy of mine really amuses people! — you really make people die of love! — this fat boy of mine how big he is — (now, tell me) whose beloved child are you? — who wants to buy a beauty! who wants to buy a beauty! — when bought and taken home he may be employed in looking after the house — never mind whether there are other people or not — it will be quite useless to shut the door with a key.

CLVIII

高高山上一個牛
四個蹄子分八辮兒
尾巴長在屁股後頭
腦袋長在脖子上頭

NOTES

辮 pan¹, the division of a hoof. The description

of this extraordinary ox will no doubt interest the reader.

TRANSLATION

On a very high mountain there is an ox — which has four hoofs and eight toes — his tail is grown under his rump — and his head is placed on his neck !

———————

CLIX

買 一 包
還 有 你 們 鬧 一 包
大 爺 吃 了 愛 撂 跤
你 們 是 撂 私 跤
你 們 是 撂 官 跤
開 着 的 跛 脚 大 箍 腰

NOTES

These words are sung by children who want to imitate the itinerant vendors of a drug for professional wrestlers, which is called 壯藥 chuang⁴ yao⁴. Is is made into black pills, called 百補增力丸 puo² pu³ tseng¹ li⁴ uan², " the hundred times forti-fying pills. 鬧 nao⁴, is not here in its original meaning but instead of 買 mai³, to buy; the expression is only used in Pekinese slang. 大爺 ta⁴ ye², vulgar appellation for a gentleman whose name and titles are unknown. 撂跤 liao¹ chiao¹, to wrestle. 私跤 ssu¹ chiao¹, wrestling among friends in a club (廠子 ch'ang³-tzu) where there is daily practice for private entertainment or with the view of entering by means of the examinations the Imperial wrestlers Corps, whose perfect and official wrestling-school is called 官跤 kuan¹ chiao¹. 開着的 k'ai¹ cho¹ ti, all this verse is composed of technical wrestling terms; this one may possibly mean to give, to play a stroke, a move. 跛脚 p'uo¹ chiao¹, to kick the adversary on the ankle in order to make him lose his balance and fall. 箍腰 ku¹ yao¹, catching the adversary by the waist to throw him to the ground by sheer superiority of strength.

CLX

初 一 初 二 初 三 四 兒
禿 媽 養 活 了 一 個 禿 寶 貝 兒
吃 禿 咂 兒
抱 禿 八 兒
禿 了 脖 梗 子
禿 腦 袋 瓜 兒

NOTES

These verses are completely devoid of any sense. 八兒 pa'r, name of the child.

TRANSLATION

On the first, on the second, on the third and on the fourth — the hairless mother has given birth to a hairless treasure — who sucks a hairless breast — she embraces the hairless young Pa — who has a hairless neck and a ha'rless head.

CLXI

你 要 奢 你 要 奢
你 要 包 金 的 大 耳 挖
等 着 搖 銅 鼓 兒 的 過 來 你 去 拏

NOTES

These words are said by mothers to little girls. The character 奢 is read here sha³ which means in country dialect what? and is used instead of the Pekinese 甚麼 shemmo³. The first form is in Peking used only in mockery. 耳挖 eur³ ua², an ear-pick. The women generally wear a silver one stuck in the hair above the left ear. Sometimes like other silver head-gears, it is gilt. 搖銅鼓兒的 iao² t'ung² ku³ 'r ti, a man who goes around in the street shaking a brass drum, and selling hair-pins, generally brass ones.

TRANSLATION

What do you want, what do you want? — you

want a big gilt ear-pick — wait till the man with the brass drum comes over and then go take it.

CLXII

開 張 把 一 爆 鞭
排 兒 邊 兩 神 財 福 增
坐 間 中 子 童 財 招
增 福 仙 增 壽 仙 劉 海 兒 本 是 海 中 仙
銀 撒 二 金 撒 一
羣 了 成 馬 騾 撒 三
樹 錢 搖 撒 四
盆 寶 聚 撒 五
順 六 六 科 登 子 五

NOTES

This rhyme is sung by boys who go round on new-year's eve to wish good luck to the families in the neighbourhood and to get the gift of some cash. The style is not altogether su-hua. 鞭炮, pienˈ p'aoˈ " whip crackers" a sort of fire-crackers which sound like the cracking of a whip. 把張開 paˈ changˈ k'aiˈ, " people open their accounts" the shops which have been shut for three, four or more days at the festival of the New-year, choose a lucky day to reopen the shop and recommence business. This ceremony is performed with solemnity and with a number of fire-crackers in proportion to the

13

importance of the shop. 增福財神 tseng¹ fu² ts'ai²
shen², "the God of wealth who increases happiness"
title of the divinity most respected by shopmen.
招財童子 chao¹ ts'ai² t'ung² tzu³. "the young man
who attracts the wealth" another divinity whose
image is pasted by shopmen on the shop door. All
the following are also names of divinities. 增福仙
tseng¹ fu² hsien¹, the Genius who increases happiness.
增壽仙 tseng¹ shou⁴ hsien¹, the Genius who length-
nes one's age. 劉海兒 liu² hai³'r, name of a
Genius supposed to bring wealth to his owner. He
is represented wearing a neck lace of gold pieces.
成了羣 ch'eng² la ch'ün², so many as to form a herd
of them. 搖錢樹 yao² ch'ien² shu⁴, a fabulous tree
whose branches are covered with gold and silver,
which falls down when one shakes the tree. 聚寶盆
chü⁴ pao³ p'en², a fabulous basin said to be possessed
in former times by a certain 沈 Shen³; this basin had
the useful quality of doubling the weight and value
of the precious metal laid in it. 登科 teng⁴ k'o¹,
to be approved at the official examinations. 六六
順 liu⁴ liu⁴ shun⁴, six times six may you have favour
(may you find every thing smooth for you).

TRANSLATION

Here is the first discharge of crackers and the
shop begins to receive customers — on both sides
is exhibited the God of wealth — and in the middle
sits " the young man who attracts wealth — there

are also the Genius of happiness, the Genius of long life and Lui-hair who is originally a genius from the sea — first let him shower gold — secondly let him shower silver — thirdly let him give you as many horses and mules as would make herds of them — fourthly let him grant you the golden-tree — fifthly let him grant you the Treasure casket — five sons all of whom shall pass the examinations and a sixfold happiness.

CLXIII

天 皇 皇
地 皇 皇
我 家 有 個 夜 哭 郎
過 往 君 子 念 三 遍
一 家 睡 到 大 天 光

NOTES

This small rhyme is sung by mothers to get children asleep and to break the evil charm which forces them to be awake. The chinese paste on the walls of the town and even in places of which no mention need be made some words which, read three times, are thought to exert a very favourable influence on the events of the day as regards the reader. These spell sentences are generally called 咒 語 chou⁴ yü³ — (the word. chou⁴, here is in a good sense, whilst in other phrases it may mean " to read incantations and spells against some body " as in the phrase 咒 罵 chou⁴ ma⁴, which means to insult and to wish bad luck to one with ready made words). — One of the most common and powerful spells is contained in the first-two verses of this rhyme, as the words which compose them are considered the most honourable of all the characters. — This spell is jokingly composed as if it were intended to be pasted on walls, and not to be sung beside the cradles of babies. 夜哭郎 ye⁴ k'u¹ lang², in nursery talk means a young gentleman who won't go to sleep.

TRANSLATION

Heaven is imperial! — The Earth is imperial — I have at home a young gentleman who weeps during the night — Let all the gentlemen who go by read these words three times — and all the family will sleep till broad daylight.

CLXIV

爺 王 竈
張 姓 本
香 炷 三 水 涼 碗 一
苦 的 混 子 小 年 今
糖 東 關 吃 再 年 明

NOTES

There are two gods of the hearth, the one is Li and is not married, the other has the surname of Chang and is married. These words are supposed to be uttered by a poor man who is performing the annual sacrifice to the God, but has not money enough to buy the sugar required for the occasion, and can only afford to prepare the bowl of water for the god's horse and three incense sticks. 小 子 hsiao³ tzu " the young man " here jocularly used for I, the undermentioned. 混 的 苦 hun¹ ti k'u³, I am living very wretchedly.

TRANSLATION

O God of the hearth — whose surname is Chang — here is a bowl of water and three incense-sticks — this year I am living very miserably — next year you shall eat the Manchurian sugar.

CLXV

灰斗灰
灰就灰
遍遍斗
進將
遍遍
進進
頭還二還三不

拿 在 手
嗬 在 口
看 你 進 斗 不 進 斗

NOTES

This rhyme is sung by boys in the street to insult opium smokers. The ways of poor opium smokers are described. These unhappy people when they have smoked the opium pill take the ashes 灰 huei¹, mix them up with saliva and make a new pill, which they place in the pipe-hole called 斗 tou³. This operation of forming a new ball with the ashes is repeated as often as three times, after which the ash of the opium loses all taste whatever. 頭遍 t'ou² pien⁴, the first time. 將就 chiang¹ chiu⁴, tolerably good, it can be used. 不進斗 pu⁴ chin¹ tou³, it means "that the ashes are no longer any good, they cannot again be pressed together to form a pill, and therefore they cannot be smoked; so they do not enter the bowl of the pipe. 嗬 this character is read an³ and nan³, and means to place something in the palm of the hand and raise it to the mouth; also to stoop down to catch hold of something with the mouth. The opium smokers chew the opium ash when it cannot be smoked any more.

TRANSLATION

The first time the ashes — may enter the bowl

of the pipe the second time — it is not so good —
and the third time — they cannot be used — then
the man rolls the ashes in his hands — and raises
them to his mouth — let us see if this time they can
enter this (new) pipe mouth.

CLXVI

三 月 三 個 有 年 年
壽 上 來 慶 娘 娘 母 王
仙 羣 會 酒 美 神 洞 各
仙 羣 會 酒 美 桃 蟠

NOTES

The third day in the third moon is the birthday
of Hsi[1]-uang[2] mu[3], the western Royal Mother, worshipped by the Chinese. 洞神 tung[1] shen[2], the Spirits
are supposed to live in grottoes. 蟠桃 p'an[2] t'ao[2]
flat peaches. 蟠桃會 p'an[2] t'ao[2] huei[4], is also called
the festival in honour of Hsi-uang[2]-mu[3], Every spirit
in attendance is supposed to be presented with a
peach. See the play called P'an-t'ao-huei. 羣仙
ch'ün[2] hsien[1], to assemble the spirits.

TRANSLATION

Every year there is the festival of the 3[d] day
of the third moon — it is the Birthday of the Royal
Mother — All the spirits in the grottoes come to

assist at the ceremony — the flat peaches and the good wine can make the spirits assemble.

CLXVII

南 京 大 柳 樹
北 京 沈 萬 三
滄 州 的 獅 子 景 州 的 塔
深 州 蜜 桃 擱 口 兒 甜

NOTES

In this rhyme are collected some of the rarities to be seen in the Empire. 沈 萬 三 Shen³ uan⁴ san¹, name of the propieter of that famous treasure-basin 聚寶盆 chü⁴ pao³ p'en² which has been spoken of before. 滄 州 Ts'ang¹ chow¹, in the Tientsin prefecture. It is stated there is an iron lion, in the interior of which there is room for ten men. 景 州 塔 ching³ chou¹ t'a³, a high pagoda in Ching-chow, in the Chihli province ; it is stated it is very high and may be seen at the distance of fifty *li*. 深 州 Shen¹ chow¹, a place renowned for its magnificent peaches. 擱 口 兒 甜 kang⁴ k'ou³ 'r t'ien², so sweet that they fill the mouth ; the same idea is also expressed by 殺 口 兒 甜 sha¹ k'ou₃ r' t'ien₂.

TRANSLATION

The willow trees in Nanking — The man Shen-uan-san in Peking — the lion in Ts'ang-chow, and the pagoda in Ching-chow — and the very sweet peaches in Shen-chow.

CLXVIII

轂洞洞
太平車
裏頭坐着個俏哥哥
城外去聽野台兒戲
回頭逛個十里河兒
老爺廟鬧吵吵
人海人山眞熱鬧
村兒裏的姑娘來賣俏
臉搽官粉賽過一個大白瓢

NOTES

轂洞洞 ku¹ tung¹ tung¹, a slang surname for a sort of travelling cart covered with a mat awning- a better name for it is 太平車 t'ai¹ p'ing² ch'o¹. 野台兒戲 ye³ t'ai² 'r hsi¹, performances on wooden stages in the country, the expense of which is paid for by means of general contributions amongst the peasants. 十里河兒 shih² li³ ho² 'r, "the ten *li* river" a brook outside the Kiang-tso-men in Peking. By its side there is a large temple in which a festival is held on the 24th of the 6th moon : its name is 老爺廟 Lao³ ye² miao¹. 鬧吵吵 nao¹ ch'ao¹ ch'ao¹, great noise and hubbub. 人海人山 jen² hai³ jen² shan¹, the men were there as thick as water and as high as hills. 寶俏 mai¹ ch'iao⁴, "to sell attractions" means "to make a display" to show off. The comparison of the girls head with the white calabash is made in mockery·

TRANSLATION

In the awning-cart — there sits a nice fellow — he is going outside the town to hear the village comedies — and then he will go down to the River of ten *li* — In the Lao-ye temple there is great confusion — the crowd is enormous, and it is very animated — the girls from the villages come here to display their charms — and their faces rubbed with white cosmetics look just like white gourds.

CLXIX

壽星老兒福祿星
增福增壽壽長生
生文生武生貲子
子孝孫賢輩輩兒榮

NOTES

This rhyme is sung by children on birthdays. The three happy stars are the 壽星 shou⁴ hsing¹, the star of longevity, 福星 fu² hsing¹, the star of happiness and 祿星 lu⁴ hsing¹, the star of appointment.

The spirit which presides over longevity is called
壽星老兒 shou¹ hsing¹ lao³ 'r.

TRANSLATION

The spirit of longevity, and the stars of happiness and appointment — may they increase your happiness and your longevity so that you may live a long life — and have sons in the literary career, in the military career and in high positions — may your sons be pious and your grandsons be for ever glorious.

CLXX

小 胖 哥
玩 藝 兒 多
搬 不 倒 兒
婆 婆 車
風 颭 燕 兒 一 大 串 兒
永 糖 葫 蘆 兒 是 果 餡 兒

NOTES

搬 不 倒 兒 pan¹ pu¹ tao³ 'r, a toy consisting of a round ball of clay on which is stuck a paper man — the plaything is so made that in whatever position one puts it, by the law of gravity it takes again its upright position. 婆 婆 車 p'uo² p'uo² ch'o¹, ladies carriage, another toy. 風 颭 燕 兒 feng¹ kua¹ yen⁴'r, another plaything in the form of a stick on which a thread is tied, not unlike a fiddestick. On this thread are fixed many paper flowers, which at the least breath of wind begin to revolve causing a peculiar whirring round. 氷 糖 葫 蘆 ping¹ t'ang² hu² lu², some fruits as the hai-t'ang are strung together by a thin stick and covered with sugar ; this is called a " sugar-gourd ".

TRANSLATION

This fat boy — has many toys — a clay puppet — and a small cart — and a great string of paper flowers — and sugar-gourds stuffed with fruits.

PEKING. — Pe-t'ang Press.